CRASH AND BURN

A DCI HARRY MCNEIL NOVEL

JOHN CARSON

DCI HARRY MCNEIL SERIES
Return to Evil
Sticks and Stones
Back to Life
Dead Before You Die
Hour of Need
Blood and Tears
Devil to Pay
Point of no Return
Rush to Judgement
Against the Clock
Fall from Grace
Crash and Burn

Where Stars Will Shine – a charity anthology compiled by Emma Mitchell, featuring a Harry McNeil short story – The Art of War and Peace

DCI SEAN BRACKEN SERIES
Starvation Lake
Think Twice
Crossing Over
Life Extinct
Over Kill

DI FRANK MILLER SERIES
Crash Point
Silent Marker
Rain Town
Watch Me Bleed
Broken Wheels
Sudden Death
Under the Knife
Trial and Error
Warning Sign
Cut Throat
Blood from a Stone
Time of Death

Frank Miller Crime Series – Books 1-3 – Box set
Frank Miller Crime Series - Books 4-6 - Box set

MAX DOYLE SERIES
Final Steps
Code Red
The October Project

SCOTT MARSHALL SERIES

Old Habits

CRASH AND BURN

Copyright © 2021 John Carson

Edited by Charlie Wilson at Landmark Editorial
Cover by Damonza

John Carson has asserted his right under the Copyright, Designs and Patents Act 1988, to be identified as the author of this work.

This is a work of fiction. Names, characters, places, brands, media, and incidents are either the products of the author's imagination or are used fictitiously. Any resemblance to actual events, locales, or persons, living or dead, is coincidental.

Without limiting the rights under copyright reserved above, no part of this publication may be reproduced, stored in or introduced into a retrieval system, or transmitted, in any form, or by any means (electronic, mechanical, photocopying, recording, or otherwise) without the prior written permission of the author of this book. Innocence is and

All rights reserved

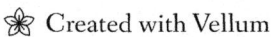

❉ Created with Vellum

For the real Lisa McDonald

ONE

The funeral had been a full police affair. Uniforms with badges, buttons and braids had been there, men Harry didn't know but who represented Scotland's finest. They had shaken his hand, told him in a compassionate voice that if he needed anything to just ask.

Women cried. Men put on their best grim faces. There were no children there, except Chance, his eighteen-year-old son, himself a police officer.

Alex's sister, Jessica, had stood beside him.

Harry had told her that he needed her by his side. She was still family, no matter what. Alex had loved her sister, Harry loved her too, and Grace would grow to love her. Harry would make sure of it.

The sun had been out the day of the funeral. It

was a still, peaceful day, and just once, a little wind had blown through the trees, a gentle breeze that had shaken the leaves for a few seconds. Harry thought it might have been Alex saying a final goodbye.

People were invited along to a local hotel where they could eat and drink and celebrate Alex's brief time on earth and share war stories. Harry would laugh, then remember where he was. Then the guilt would kick him for his not remembering that his wife was gone. He shouldn't forget it for one second, but he knew he would. Not entirely, but as time carried him forward, there would be times throughout the day when he wouldn't think about Alex.

Then, after the funeral, the disbelief slowly turned to anger. How fucking dare she leave him to go somewhere else? She had no right doing that at all. What the hell was she thinking, going off like that, leaving a baby behind?! How was he going to cope on his own? How was he going to hold down a job and take care of a baby by himself?

'You know, Harry, you're angry because she left you. I mean, who would have the balls to leave Harry McNeil? He's a tough copper who deserves to have his wife waitin' at home for him. Hell, I'd be angry if my wife left me. After a while, you'll feel the anger ease. It wasn't Alex's fault that she died.'

Harvey Levitt was an American and the force's psychologist. He worked for the University of Edinburgh, but that day, he was working with Harry.

At that point, Harry was only half listening. The other half of his brain was spinning round and round so that everything was distorted. His life had been derailed and was lying on its side in a ditch, and all the King's horses and all the King's men were fucked if they knew how to put him back together again.

TWO

Thunder cracked overhead. *With a bit of luck, I might be struck down by a finger of lightning out to poke somebody's head in,* Harry McNeil thought.

It was lashing down outside, but all Harry was interested in was getting wet inside. 'One for the road,' he said to Scramble, the barman and co-owner of the Thistle Hotel.

'You said that two pints ago, Harry, son,' Scramble replied, digging out a clean pint glass anyway. 'I don't want to be giving you a colly bucky all the way up the road.'

'What's a colly bucky?' said a young woman a few bar stools down.

'A piggyback ride. You know, getting some

drunken sod on your back and carrying them home. But kids play it too. Mind you, in this day and age, they might be pished as well.'

'That's a bleak outlook on life, Scramble,' Harry said. *At least I have an excuse.*

'It's true, though,' Scramble replied, beginning to pour the pint. Harry knew if he had been swaying and slurring his words, Scramble would have punted him out the door with the tip of his boot, but Harry had assured him he wasn't driving and the walk up to his cottage would sober him up no end. That, and the pissing rain and driving wind.

'It is true,' the woman said. 'I should know: I started drinking when I was fifteen.' She was in her late thirties and was a regular in the bar. Chloe Walker. Harry had been introduced to her one night, and he'd already been half-jaked at the time, well on his way to being full-jaked, if there was such a thing. First impressions hadn't put her off having a laugh with him in the bar at night.

Scramble put the glass down on the bar and Harry handed over some notes. 'One for yourself there, my friend.'

'I thought I was your friend?' Chloe said, grinning at him.

Harry shrugged. 'One for my other friend too,' he said, handing over more money.

'It's not true what they say about you, Harry,' Scramble said, pouring a Bacardi for Chloe.

'It is true, more than you'll ever know.' Harry raised his glass at his new friends and Chloe raised hers in salute.

'I'll put one in the till for later,' Scramble said.

Harry had only been here for two weeks when he'd been invited to the lock-in after hours. He vaguely remembered enjoying himself, being taken under the wing of the other regulars. They were his new friends now, and their friendship had been cemented that Sunday night. That was almost three months ago.

Chloe added the remnants from her Coke can, the Bacardi getting a head on it for a few brief seconds. 'That was a bit of a laugh last night, wasn't it?' she said to him.

'It was. I haven't had such a laugh in a long time.'

'I hadn't been to the bowling club in ages.'

A thought of his own bowling club back in Edinburgh flashed into Harry's mind, but like an errant Messerschmitt, he shot it down in flames. Like he did with most thoughts of his old city these days.

'I'm surprised you didn't put your back out in that conga line, Harry,' Scramble said. Being the owner of the bar meant Scramble let his manager take the helm on a Saturday night, so he himself could let his hair down. What was left of it.

'I practised all week,' Harry said, knocking back more of the lager.

'You're a dark horse,' Chloe said, smiling at him.

'Aye, still waters and all that,' Scramble said.

'Any more clichés?' Harry said, looking over the rim of his glass at the old man sitting in the corner of the pub. He was pretending to read a newspaper but was always looking over at Harry and then averting his eyes. A nosy local? Harry didn't think so, or else he would have noticed him in here before. Wouldn't he?

A man came up to the bar and ordered a couple of pints. 'How do, Harry?' he said as Scramble started pouring the pints.

'Hair of the dog, Alan. How about you?'

'I'm not as fit as you, son. My wife likes dancing, but my knee gave up that ghost a long time ago. She said to buy you a drink for keeping an old woman happy. Wee nip?'

'Aye, go on then, pal. And tell Jean it was my

pleasure. I can dance like a brick can swim, but my enthusiasm is there, if not my skill.'

'Wee nip for the boy here, Scramble,' Alan said. 'I tell you, it made me break out in a sweat just seeing you dancing out there, Harry.'

'Aye, well, I was having just as much fun as Jean.' Harry took the whisky from Scramble and clinked his glass with Alan's. 'Thank you for letting me slip into your community and treating me like a friend and not a stranger.'

'Not like the old boy who's been watching you all night,' Alan said, taking a sip of his lager. They both looked over to where the old man had been sitting, but he was gone, the newspaper left folded on his table.

'Another stranger passing through,' Harry said, not meaning it.

'I doubt it, son. He's been in here before, so he must be staying somewhere. God knows where. It's not in any official place and nobody seems to know him. Which is unusual. My wife knows everything about everybody, but I haven't heard her talking about that old boy.'

Harry looked at the contents of his glass for a moment. *I bet she doesn't know everything about me.*

'Maybe he's just quiet. Wants to be left in peace.' Harry didn't believe his own words.

'We'll see. Take care, son.' Alan lifted the other pint, then went back to the table where his friend was waiting for his lager.

Harry poured the whisky into his pint glass and looked around the bar. It was small but comfortable and always busy on a Sunday, as if nobody had got the message that tomorrow was Monday and a work day.

Chloe was an artist and worked in her own studio on the same little private road he lived on, and Harry wondered how she could lift a brush to the canvas in the mornings. Or maybe she was like him and slept in until lunchtime.

Some of the others had asked him what he did for a living and he had replied that he was an entrepreneur. Most people left it at that, having no idea what one of those was but guessing he made money from it. How else would he be able to afford living here without driving a tractor?

He made small talk with Scramble before he called for last orders.

'Not for me; that was my one for the road, remember?' Harry said to the older man.

'Aye, well, thanks to your insatiable thirst, I'll be

able to take my wife to the Caribbean for a winter holiday.'

'Tell her to send me a postcard,' Harry said, finishing off the dregs in his glass before grabbing his jacket from the coat stand and heading off.

Thunder cracked, louder this time, or was it just because he was outside that it seemed louder? Lightning frazzled the sky as the rain fell down like somebody had forgotten to turn the water heater on. He pulled up the collar on his jacket, the rain soaking his hair.

That was another thing he was reminded of in the bathroom mirror each morning: his hair was longer and he had stopped shaving. Trimming his beard was way easier than dragging a sliver of steel over his face every day. Why would he bother with that nonsense anyway? It wasn't like he had anywhere to go.

He headed off along Wigtown Road, the shops in darkness now, waiting for the morning's customers. The chippie was open of course, so he ducked in for a poke of chips and made small talk with the man behind the counter while his chips were wrapped.

Back outside again, the rain couldn't dampen how good the chips tasted.

'Harry.' He heard the voice right behind him. He

recognised it as female, which meant nothing: he'd had a good belting off a woman before as he'd tried to take her into custody. But there wasn't an undertone of a threat there.

He turned to see Chloe standing there looking at him. She was holding an umbrella over her head, but her denim jacket was still absorbing the weather like a sponge.

'If it's one of my chips you want, I have to warn you, I always have salt and sauce.'

'It's not your chips I want,' she said, picking one out of the brown paper wrapper anyway. 'Jesus, they're hot.'

'Not for long.' He held out a hand, palm up, to indicate that the weather would soon take care of cooling down the chips.

'Share a taxi with me. You'll catch your death.'

That's the whole point.

'It's not that far to walk.'

'Rubbish. We live on the same road, Harry.'

'The walk will do me good.'

'Come on, don't be daft. Old Man Hemingway just got in his taxi. Somebody else will take it if we don't jump in.'

Old Man Hemingway, like the writer, had come back from the dead and was now driving a taxi in southern Scotland instead of writing a new masterpiece. Harry could see the man sitting in the car outside the taxi office next to the chippie, waiting for somebody to part with the hard-earned, having left just enough for him after renting some beer in the bar across the road.

'Aye, go on then. Why not?' Harry said, offering Chloe another chip.

Chloe put her fingers into her mouth and whistled loudly, putting her other hand out. It was a skill that Harry could never master, no matter how hard he tried. Putting a hand out, yes – the whistling bit, no. He wondered if it came naturally, or did people practise it? Either way, it was hardly needed since the taxi office was next door to the chippie, but then the whistle laid claim to the car.

Hemingway looked in his rear-view mirror and saw it wasn't some wido who was pished and would fall asleep in the back. Harry held the back door open while Chloe fiddled with her umbrella, pressing a button to fold it. She scooted across the back seat and Harry was about to get in when Hemmingway stopped him.

'No food, drink or smoking, squire,' he said.

'It's just a few chips, Ken,' Chloe said.

Harry was oddly relieved that the man's name wasn't Ernest.

'I suppose you'll want to come back in the morning to wipe the puke off the mats in the back when he's finished tossing his bag?' Hemingway said.

Chloe looked awkwardly between Harry and the taxi driver like there was a standoff going on. Hemingway had shot from the hip and now the only victim was Harry's poke of chips.

'The only thing being tossed is these chips,' Harry said, and he got back out of the car.

'A moment on the lips, a lifetime on the hips anyway,' Chloe said as he climbed out, as if she was looking at his arse.

He threw the wrapper and chip remnants into the bin outside the chippie, then got back in out of the rain. 'Those were an early breakfast,' he said.

'To the studio, Ken, please,' she said, and the old man knew where to go. Harry wondered what he should call his own place – that white dump up on the hillside outside of town?

The car turned and headed back the way they had come, from the hotel's bar.

'You could have walked and been home quicker,' Harry said.

'No, I couldn't. Besides, there could have been some deviant walking about.'

'I thought you told me you carried a knife with you?' Harry said, grinning.

Hemingway looked in his mirror at them, wondering if he was going to get rolled. He picked up his radio handset and spoke into it, telling the despatcher – his long-suffering wife – where he was going and who was in the taxi. They might find his rotting corpse in a field after a frenzied attack, but at least they'd know who to look for.

It was a five-minute drive back along the main road. Harry thought that everywhere in Newton Stewart was a five-minute drive. Over the roundabout and Hemingway took a right, going up a track that was knocking on the door of being a road if Harry and Chloe decided to splash out on some tarmacadam.

Chloe's cottage was on the right. Nice piece of property, surrounded by a small fence and flowers bordering a well-kept front lawn. A detached garage was off to one side.

'Nightcap?' she asked Harry.

'Well...'

'Oh, go on. Or you could get Ken to drive you to

your front door, then sneak back down so he doesn't spread some gossip.'

'Doesn't matter to me what you two do in your own time. But make up your mind, for God's sake. They'll be pouring out of the pub shortly and I don't want the drunken sods walking home. It'll be going like a fair tonight.'

Chloe put her hand in her small bag.

'I'll get this,' Harry said.

'I know. I was just getting my keys out.' She laughed and got out the car, popping her umbrella up again.

Harry gave Ken a good tip and got out into what he thought must have been the tail end of a hurricane. He sprinted round the car and got close to Chloe under her umbrella.

'You're going to need a bigger umbrella,' he said, thinking of the line from the *Jaws* movie.

She put an arm around him as if squeezing him under and they trotted up to her front door in a kind of half-pished foxtrot, which consisted of stumbling and ducking and, in Harry's case, trying not to slip and fall on his arse.

Chloe got her key out and opened the front door and they went in. She held the umbrella out of the front door and shook it a bit before closing the door.

She hit a light switch and they walked along the lobby. The rain had brought with it a drop in temperature and the house felt cool.

Too cool.

Chloe looked at Harry. The rain seemed loud, and not a *hitting the roof* kind of loud.

She stepped into the kitchen and stopped. 'Jesus. There's somebody in the house.'

THREE

The window was open and there were muddy footprints on the floor, trailing out into the lobby.

'Stay here,' he said, about to leave the kitchen.

'I might be a woman, Harry, but I don't back away from anything.'

He nodded at her. 'Fair enough.'

'Hand me a knife.'

'Which one? Flick or Stanley?'

'The big one,' she said, reaching around him. She took the biggest knife from the butcher's block on the counter and walked away with it.

Yes, your honour, I was there when she gave him a good belting, just before she fatally stabbed him. In self-defence, mind. Or maybe he'd just say, *I saw fuck all.*

He followed her, now noticing the muddy footprints on the dark carpet. Chloe went into the first room, the living room. All clear. Then the bedrooms, and finally her bathroom, before going through to her home studio.

'Whoever it was, he's long gone,' Harry said. 'Maybe just a transient hoping to find your family jewels.'

'I'll cut *his* family jewels off if I catch him,' she said, and Harry thought he could feel tears springing to his eyes.

'Just make sure you lock up before I go.'

She turned to him so fast, he thought she was going to stab him. 'You're not leaving just now, are you?' She saw him eyeing the knife and laughed. 'Sorry. I'm not going to hold you hostage. You're free to leave any time you want to.'

'I'll close your kitchen window and put the kettle on while I'm there.' He walked back to the kitchen and flicked the light off, gently closing the door behind him. He walked up to the window, closed it and peered out into the night, but there was nothing there but a cloying darkness. If somebody was out there watching them, then he still had the advantage, even though Harry was standing in the darkened room.

'You think he's out there?' Chloe asked, right behind him now. Anybody else's heart might have jumped like it had starter cables attached to it, but Harry had been in too many situations where somebody had tried to creep up on him, and he had heard the faint sound of the kitchen door opening. Plus the light from the hallway was firmly reflected on the kitchen window, illuminating them both.

'It's pissing down, dark and cold, and he would be on a slippery hill, so I'm going to take a guess at no.' He pulled the roller blind down and turned to her as she walked over to hit the light switch.

'Coffee or hot chocolate?' she asked him.

'Hot chocolate. Otherwise I'll be up all night.'

She smiled at him and he could see she was about to make a crack, but she turned to the kettle instead.

He looked at her back, at her slim figure and blonde hair, and thought she could almost pass for Alex. The image jolted him for a moment and he almost took off, but he sat down at the kitchen table instead.

'Help yourself to a biscuit,' she said, but he didn't know where they were, so he stayed seated.

'I'm fine, thanks,' he said, not sure if a chocolate

digestive would mix with what few chips he'd managed to scran.

She opened a cupboard and took out a packet of Hobnobs. Harry mentally kicked himself for refusing, willing to take the risk now. She put the packet on the table and poured the hot water into two mugs and added milk.

'Maybe just one,' he said, taking the clothes peg off the wrapper.

'Keeps them fresh,' Chloe explained as she saw him holding the peg.

'Pegs are multi-tools,' he said after swallowing the first bite. 'They can hang your skids on the line, then when you're done with that, they can keep your biscuit packet closed. Who knew?'

She laughed as she brought the mugs over and sat at the table with him. 'I don't know about you, but I never hang my skids out on the line,' she said.

Harry drank some of the hot chocolate, which tasted surprisingly good. If he had gone home on his own, he would have been sitting with a single malt by now, but this was a close second.

'I just burn mine and order more from Amazon,' he said, taking another biscuit from the packet. 'I'll bring you more when I come round next time,' he said after his mouth was empty.

'Make sure you do, Harry Mackay.'

He looked at her for a second, just a fleeting second, wondering why she was calling him Mackay. Then he remembered: this was who he was down here. Mackay was one of his middle names, and he had used that as soon as he got down to the small town. Nobody had to know who he was. Just some businessman down here fixing up the old cottage he'd bought.

'I might even splash out and bring in some Tunnock's Tea Cakes.'

'Big spender, eh? But I only have one or two. Have to watch my figure, you know.'

'You're doing a good job of it so far,' he said, but that sounded too much like flirting and he felt ice flowing through his veins at the thought.

'Big spender. Smooth talker. What other tricks do you have up your sleeve, Harry?' She grinned and took a sip of her hot chocolate.

'You'll just have to wait and see.'

Chloe put the mug down on the table. 'I was wondering if you would like to join me for a drink on my birthday? Maybe have a bite to eat in town. Or go up to Ayr. Somewhere different.'

Harry looked at her to see if there was any hidden meaning there, but if she was holding a stacked deck, then he couldn't see it.

'Aye, that would be great. When is it?'

'Next Saturday.'

'Smashing, aye. Maybe Ayr then, unless you fancy a bag of chips from our usual chippie?'

'Oh, I don't think I could take that much fun.' She laughed again, and he saw a brightness in her eyes. He wondered what she saw when she looked into his eyes, if she even did look into his eyes. Would she see the hurt there, the wishing that he was dead sometimes? The pain that he felt would rip his insides out sometimes?

'I'll pay, of course,' she added, and he realised he had been quiet for a moment. 'Since it was my idea.'

Harry snapped out of it. 'What? Oh no, that's fine. My treat. Sorry, I was miles away. What are you in the mood for?'

'I know a nice little Chinese place.'

'Chinese it is. You can book it under my name and I'll take care of it.'

'You don't have to. I wasn't hinting for you to pay,' she said, and he could see she meant it.

'I know you weren't.' Sometimes it seemed like she had a permanent smile on her face. It was something he liked about her.

'I know you're probably wondering how old I'll be,' she said.

'Twenty-one?' he said.

'Oh, you really know how to play this game, don't you?' she said, laughing again. 'Guessing somebody's age is like buying a second-hand car: you lowball, then when you find out the higher figure, you feign surprise and say, *Really?* But I'm a wee bit older than twenty-one, and if you say fifty, I won't have you round for hot chocolate anymore.'

Harry looked at her. 'Forty,' he said.

'Yes! That was a good guess.'

'I didn't guess. Scramble told me in the bar the other night.'

'I know. He told me he had told you. So now we've got that out of the way, how old are you?'

'I'm twenty-one. Almost.'

'Ah, I see. Delusional, with a side order of narcissism.'

'That's not very nice,' Harry said.

She smiled. 'How about double?'

He smiled back at her and nodded. 'Almost. Forty-two in a couple of weeks.'

'Wonderful! We should make it a double celebration.'

He put up a hand. 'No. The big four-oh is a

unique birthday. I can celebrate being forty-two any year. This will be for you only.'

'That's very kind, but I'd rather celebrate the dying days of my thirties.'

'Then let's do that. Tomorrow night in the bar we can let our hair down.'

'Wouldn't that just be like every other night, Harry?'

'You've got a point there.' He finished his chocolate, then stood up. 'You still got that whistle you told me about?'

'I have, but the wind may carry away the sound. You're up the hill.'

'I thought you were going to say *over the hill*. I'm only just celebrating the dying days of being forty-one,' he said, raising an eyebrow and smiling.

'I meant your house.'

'It's only a two-minute walk downhill to here. Call me if you need me.' *My disposable phone will ring, because that's the only number I gave you.*

'I will.'

She walked him to the door. 'Here, take my umbrella. Bring it down tomorrow when you pop in for a coffee.'

'I'm popping in for a coffee, am I?'

'You are now,' she said, nodding to the umbrella.

'Lock your door,' he said, stepping out into the rain and putting the umbrella up. He thought himself lucky that it didn't have flowers on it but was black.

This being a private road, it didn't have any street lights, but Harry's eyes adjusted to the darkness through the lashing rain. The umbrella was barely managing to keep his hair dry, but it meant his eyes were open wider.

After a few of months of living here, he knew every little turn, knew where the dangerous stones were that could trip up an unwary person in the dark and would certainly give a mountain goat a run for its money.

That's why he saw the kitchen window open on the side of his house.

FOUR

He kept to the side of his gravel driveway and walked on the grass, which was wild now but he was hoping would form some sort of lawn in the future.

He moved fast, the rain and the walk uphill conspiring to sober him up. He wasn't sure if the black umbrella would somehow stick out in the dark, but he ditched it anyway and crouched into a run towards the side of his house.

One of the first things Harry had done was employ a painter to come along and paint the outside of the house white after a contractor had made sure the rest of the house was weatherproof. It meant he could see somebody standing outside against the white backdrop if he came home in the dark and somebody was waiting for him.

Like now.

But there was nobody there so far as he could see. He made his way around the two-storey home, ducking under the windows, until he'd come full circle and was back at the open kitchen window.

He stopped and listened, but if anybody was inside, they might have seen him coming. He waited, the rain seemingly coming down harder, sizzling off the grass and the trees and bushes on the hillside, the wind helping the rain to batter his house. He was soaked through now, but kept listening, not moving. If anybody was inside, maybe they would think they were imagining things or would want to come out to see where he was.

Then he heard it, faint but distinct.

A dog was barking, further up the hill.

The road led up and around a bend, where a house had once stood until it burned down and became derelict. That had been twenty-odd years ago, apparently, and now there was just an open space where the house had been.

He wondered if he had imagined it, but then it came again.

There was a farm down the hill and over, and it could have been one of their dogs, but it sounded like it was coming from the derelict place.

He pushed his kitchen window shut as best he could, then made his way back over to the road. The hill behind his house was steep and he didn't want to fall and break a leg, so going up the road and keeping to the side where the trees were was the safest bet.

He didn't intend on tackling anybody at first, should anybody be there, but the thought of somebody breaking into his house pissed him off. However, he couldn't be sure he had left the windows locked, and he had known some young guys who would have been more than capable of gaining entry with no problem at all.

He crested the hill and walked through the trees to the edge of the old property, and then he heard it, much more clearly now: the dog barked again.

It was coming from the old van parked in what had once been a parking space for the house.

Harry had taken a walk up here when he had first moved in. There was a wall that was once part of the house but was now overgrown and only waist high.

Harry ducked as he came out of the trees and ran over to the van in the rain. There were no lights on so far as he could see and the engine wasn't running.

If there was somebody inside then they would know he was here now as the dog started barking continuously. As plans went, this wasn't one of his better ones. The dog didn't sound very big, but sometimes the smaller dogs were more vicious than the big ones.

Then one of the van's doors opened. 'Is that you, Grandad?' a young woman said.

Harry stood there looking at her and the dog she had on a lead started going berserk.

He was about to say, *No, it isn't Grandad*, when a voice answered in the affirmative, just as a steel barrel was put against his back. Then Harry smiled at the woman, and a battery-powered storm lantern came on. A child's face peered out from a sleeping bag, the eyes framed in glasses. The dog settled down and started wagging its tail.

'Move and I'll blow you away, you big streak o' piss,' the voice said. Grandad, he presumed.

Harry laughed.

'What's so funny?' the man asked.

'You,' Harry said, turning round. 'I've had a shotgun put into my back before and that isn't one.'

He saw the old man holding a piece of pipe. He was smaller and thinner than Harry. 'Where's Snow White and the other six?'

'Cheeky bastard. I could still give you a belting with it.'

'You could try,' Harry said, 'or you could explain to me why you broke into the houses down there. But then again, that doesn't really need any explaining, does it? You're a transient thief.'

He saw the man raise the bar slightly. He made the sort of face somebody makes when walking through a cobweb.

'You wouldn't even get it raised high enough to strike before I knocked you out,' Harry said.

'You hear that, Lisa?' the man said to the woman. 'Threatening an old man with violence. And a smaller man at that. What's life coming to?'

'To be fair, you did threaten him with your pretend shotgun.'

'I'm outnumbered, I can tell.' The man threw the pipe into the van and looked at the dog, who started barking again. 'Bella! Enough. Good girl.'

Bella sniffed his hand and started wagging her tail.

The old man nodded for Lisa to take the dog further into the high-top van.

'What kind of dog is she? She looks like a Lemon Beagle.' The dog did indeed look like a Beagle, but she was white with brown patches on her, one in the middle of her back like a little saddle.

'She's a Beagle mix, the dog shelter said.' The

man looked more closely at Harry. 'You're the fella who lives down in the first white house.' It was a statement more than a question. 'Come in, son, and we'll get the coffee on.'

'This is a first for me, getting asked inside the back of a van by a couple of housebreakers.' Harry stepped inside, not feeling threatened by any of them in the slightest. Especially the little girl, who had popped her head back up again. He could see she had Down's Syndrome and was very young.

'Hello,' she said to him. 'My name's Alice. What's yours?'

Harry wondered if he'd slipped down the rabbit hole for a moment: an old man, a young woman, a girl and a dog all walked into a bar. No, he couldn't even have made this up.

There was clutter, but it was organised clutter.

'Harry.' He looked at the little girl and smiled.

'This is Maisy.' A stuffed animal came out of its hiding place in the sleeping bag. 'Say hello.'

'Hello, Maisie.' He looked at the woman. 'I know your name is Lisa. I don't know the old man's name,' he said as Grandad climbed in and shut the door.

'Oh, well done. Now he knows my name,' Lisa said.

'Less of the bloody old,' Grandad said to Harry.

'You *are* bloody old,' Lisa said. 'You're lucky Harry here didn't round on you and give you a stiff kicking.'

'Aye, that wouldn't have gone down well with my arthritis right enough.' Grandad was short enough that he could stand inside the high top without bending, but Harry could feel his head touching the roof.

'You got a name?' Harry asked. He could see the cogwheels turning in the old man's head, as if he was having a run-up to another wisecrack.

'Liam McDonald. That's my granddaughter, Lisa McDonald. And we're not bloody housebreakers.'

'I think he already got that,' Lisa replied, but there was no anger in her voice. She had rolled the dice by opening the back of the van, and if the man creeping about in the dark and the rain turned out to be a psycho, then it was too late.

'Liam, Lisa and Alice. And not forgetting Bella. Sounds like a travelling circus.'

'You're full of the wit, aren't you?' Liam said.

Harry clicked his fingers. 'I saw you down in the bar tonight.' He saw Lisa was about to pour some water into a small pan and light a camping stove. 'No, no, don't bother. Thanks for the offer anyway.' He looked at the little girl, and in his mind the van had exploded and they were all lying in the rain, waiting for the weather to cool their burning skin.

'It's no problem,' Lisa said.

It is if we all want to live. Harry was tense. He still had enough of the drink in him to go boxing should the old man and the young woman have a go. No doubt the adrenaline was zooming around, creating the same cocktail of hooligan juice that bolstered many a man in a pub every weekend.

He looked at Liam, soaked through to the skin. What thinning hair he had left was plastered to his skull, and for the first time, Harry noticed that the old man wasn't even wearing a jacket but a dark sweater. Lisa had been wet; her hair was damp, but it was obvious she had dried it.

'Let me guess: Liam was down in the pub keeping an eye on me and' – he was about to say her name but stopped himself – 'the woman who lives down the hill, while you, Lisa, went in the houses to check them out. Does that sound about right?'

'Aye,' Liam said. 'That was the plan, but two things happened: Lisa realised the house was occupied and she saw headlights coming up the hill, so she scarpered back to the van.'

'I wouldn't have broken into your house. The last time we were here, it was empty and nothing was locked. We're not housebreakers; we're just looking for somebody. Somebody who's missing. I promise you we didn't go into the houses. Grandad just went down to the pub to ask if somebody was living in your house. We don't want to do anything illegal.'

'Where was Alice?'

'In here with Bella. Nobody would get near her, trust me,' Lisa said, but Harry could tell that not even the young woman totally believed that. So they had been acting out of desperation.

'Who's missing?' Harry asked.

Lisa looked to the old man before looking Harry in the eye. 'It doesn't matter. He's not here. We're just wasting our time again.'

'Do you have any ID on you?' he asked Liam.

'What, are you a copper now?'

'I'm just a local businessman who was minding his own business until somebody broke into his house.'

'She just told you we didn't break in. Attention span of the dog there.'

Lisa nodded to her grandfather. Liam tutted but brought out a tattered old wallet. He showed his driving licence to Harry.

'Now, if you're thinking of dropping us in it with

the police, we haven't broken any laws. Lisa maybe, with trespassing, but Alice and I are squeaky clean.'

'Throwing me under the bloody bus,' Lisa said. 'I might tell them about your stash of weed and the illegal handgun you have.'

'What?' Liam spluttered. 'Don't be talking like that! He might believe you!'

Lisa smiled. 'Relax, I'm kidding.'

'I never put your mother over my knee when she was a bairn, and it's clear she didn't do it with you either. If my bloody back wasn't so bad...' He left the statement open, indicating that Lisa had got off lightly.

Harry knew he should call the police, but he was a good judge of character and these people didn't look like they were hardened criminals.

'If what you say is true, then there's nothing to report.' He looked at their feet: they were wearing trainers. The prints in Chloe's kitchen came from thick-soled boots, probably a size eleven by the look of it.

'How about I take you down to my house where you can get warmed up.' *And have a cup of coffee without blowing us all up.*

Liam looked at Lisa.

'Can we, Mum?' Alice said. 'Maisie's getting cold.'

Lisa hesitated for a moment, then Harry jumped in. 'Come on. I'm assuming this van will start?'

'Of course it will. Do you think we pushed it all the way up the hill?' Liam said.

'Grandad!' Lisa said. 'I don't know about you, but I don't want the offer taken back.' She looked at Harry. 'Thank you, Harry. I'd love a cup of coffee.'

'You can have a shower too. All of you can. I have spare beds. But you already knew that.' He looked at Liam, who made a face and shook his head.

'Yes, I know the layout of your house. I was in it when it was empty. But we're law-abiding citizens.'

'Come on then. Your daughter needs a decent bed for the night,' Harry said to Lisa.

'Just so you know,' Lisa said, 'if he *was* one of the Dwarfs, he'd be *Farty*.'

'Did you say *Forty*?' Liam asked.

'Yeah, that was it.'

FIVE

He lay further up on the hillside, the rain beating down on his waterproofs. These weren't your average hiking waterproofs bought online, made in China by a schoolgirl on her lunch break. These were the real deal. They meant he could lie in the pissing rain knowing nothing was going to get in.

Same with the night-vision binoculars: they cost a pretty penny, but you had to invest in good materials when you were in his line of work. Some men got careless and over-confident and that often led to their demise. Not him. He was not going to go out because he had made a stupid mistake.

He watched the old van trundle down the hill towards the white house and the glare of the red brake lights as they cut through the dark and the rain.

This might be a problem. The man in the white house, and not the clown over in America, stepped out of the back of the van with the woman and the child. The dog followed, running across to the front door as if it knew where it was going.

Then the old man got out from behind the wheel after putting the lights out.

Then they all went into the house.

He got up and put his binoculars away and started walking in the opposite direction.

He would wait and see if they needed to be taken care of.

SIX

They took their wet coats off in the mudroom at the side of the house. It was warm in here, a space where muddy boots and wet jackets could come off. And where dogs could shake their coats before running into the main room and rubbing themselves on the furniture.

Bella didn't disappoint and ran through to the living room in search of a blanket, which she found on Harry's couch. She jumped up, rolled onto her back with her legs in the air and shuffled from side to side.

'Bella!' Lisa shouted, rushing after the dog, who was grunting in pleasure. Lisa tried to coax the dog off, but Harry grabbed some towels from a cupboard in the mudroom, including one for the dog, and dished them out.

'Just a small one for me, obviously,' Liam said. 'Since I'm a midget.'

'Just take it, Grandad, and think yourself lucky.' Lisa managed to get the dog off the couch and Bella wandered over to the log fire, which was dying on its feet.

'It's no problem,' Harry said, towelling his short hair. Bella stood and barked at something that only she could hear. Harry put some more logs on the fire. 'I have central heating too, but it's good to dry off in front of the real fire.'

Fifteen minutes later, they were dry, the kettle had just gone off the boil, and both the dog and Alice were dozing. Lisa came back down the stairs after making up the two beds in the spare rooms.

'Alice will be in with me,' Lisa said, 'and Grandad, you'll be in your own room. I can't thank you enough, Harry.'

'No problem. I've made a brew.'

'Not for me,' Liam said. 'There's only a fifty per cent chance that I won't get up for a pee.'

'The other fifty per cent is he'll piss the bed,' Lisa said.

'Steady. I haven't peed in the van, have I?'

'Give it time.' Lisa shook her head. 'I'm going to sit down with Harry and a nice cup of coffee. I think he deserves an explanation, don't you?'

The old man agreed he did.

Then there was a knock on the front door.

'You expecting anyone?' Liam asked.

'No,' Harry said, walking over to one of the windows and looking out at the figure standing under the outside light. He answered it and showed his new guest inside. Bella started barking until Lisa assured her it was okay.

'Folks, this is Chloe Walker,' Harry said, making the introductions. Chloe had taken down her umbrella; Harry wondered if she had a collection of them in the house since he still had her other one. Technically, it was in his front garden somewhere, but he was still classed as the borrower.

'Charmed, I'm sure,' Liam said, grinning and holding out a hand, barely restraining himself from going in for a hug.

'Nice to meet you,' she replied.

'We're about to have coffee,' Harry said. 'Would you like to join us?'

'I don't want to interrupt anything,' Chloe said. 'I just came round to see if you can still make it for coffee tomorrow.' Meaning, she came round to see if she should go call the police.

Harry moved in close. 'I'll take your coat.' Then he leaned in even closer. 'You saw the van and wanted to make sure I was alright.'

'You make me feel like an old gossip, Harry Mackay.'

'I would never dare suggest such a thing.' He introduced the others, then took her coat and walked through to the mudroom.

'I'll help with the coffee,' Chloe said to Lisa and they went through to the kitchen.

Harry went back into the house. The little dog wagged her tail at him, then Chloe and Lisa came back into the room with coffee mugs. Lisa went back for the milk and sugar.

'The wee yin's away to bed,' Liam said. 'I appreciate you letting us stay here, but we'll be away in the morning.'

'Nobody's shoving you out, Liam.'

'Nobody wants to overstay their welcome, son. Besides, tomorrow it's off to work we go.'

Lisa looked at Harry and shook her head at the Snow White reference.

'We're constantly moving,' she said.

'Not that we're gypsies,' Liam jumped in. 'The van is our mobile command centre.'

'You're just digging a deeper hole here, Grandad,' Lisa said, and Harry could see the tiredness in her eyes. He wondered when she had last got a decent night's sleep.

'Listen, why don't we sit down and you can tell me about this missing person you mentioned.'

They sat down, Lisa sitting on the couch next to Chloe. A fresh blanket had been draped over the back and she puffed up a pillow, ready for the big campfire story.

'It was a year ago now...'

SEVEN

One year earlier

'I said no, Jack!' Lisa McDonald slammed the iron down onto the board.

'He'll like it,' Jack Easton said. 'Mind when I used to take him on the train all the time? He loved it. Eh, wee man?'

Henry McDonald stood looking at his sister. 'I love the trains,' he said, then went back to looking down at the floor, where something far more interesting was happening. At seventeen, Henry was awkward, but he had Asperger's Syndrome and Lisa knew this was to be expected. She knew he would be able to get a job that worked with his disability, and she was sure Henry would love it, and she had been told there would be a position available for him. But not if Jack was intent on taking him away trainspotting for a couple of days.

'He's going to the leisure centre tomorrow.'

'Oh, what? Swimming's for lassies.'

'Don't tell him that. He loves swimming.' This was just another example of why they had got divorced, Lisa thought.

'Can you play with my doll, Dad?' Alice said, coming up to her dad, holding two dolls, one for him.

'Later, sweetheart,' he said, ruffling her hair. Alice turned away from him and went back to the settee, where she was playing with her dolls.

'Oh, come on, Lisa. I promised Henry yonks ago that I would take him, but I've only just got time off now.'

'You're a journalist. You can take as much time off as you like,' she said as steam hissed out of the hot iron.

'You think it's like that? I'm offended. I work weird hours, you know that. We might not still be married, but I like to pay my way. So I work a lot of hours.'

'I don't know, Jack. What if Henry doesn't like it?'

Jack beamed a smile at her. 'He'll love it. Eh, pal? We'll take loads of photos, and then when the Flying Scotsman comes next, we'll go and see that.' He nodded to Henry, who stood looking at the floor.

'Why don't you take Alice?' Lisa asked.

Jack looked at Alice, his smile slipping for just a moment. Lisa could see the man behind the mask.

'Maybe next time,' he said.

Lisa knew he was embarrassed by his daughter and would rather spend time with Henry, Lisa's brother, than his own daughter.

'It's always next time with you.'

'I will, I promise.'

'You'd better look after him, Jack. I'm not kidding.'

'I will.' Jack smiled at her. 'We're going to have fun, eh, Henry?'

'Yes. We're going to look at the trains.' A faint smile worked its way onto Henry's face.

'Right, get cracking then, lad. Pack a backpack with some skids and a fresh shirt or two, then we'll be off.'

Henry scuttled away to his room.

'It wouldn't kill you to play with your daughter once in a while,' Lisa said.

'I will. When she wants to go out and play football or something. You know I'm not a dolls man.' He kept his voice low and looked over at Alice playing by herself on the settee.

'But you'll go and watch trains with my brother?'

'I will. Henry's a good lad.'

'Just don't get him too excited. And don't take your eye off him. You know he goes into those silent moods and wanders off.'

'We're going to look at trains. More for the lad than me. So he'll be watching the trains and I'll be watching out for him.'

Henry came back into the room with his battered old suitcase. He'd seen it in a charity shop window and had wanted it, so Lisa had bought it for him. Since their mum and died had died, she and his grandpa were his only family, along with Alice.

'Mind and do as Uncle Jack tells you, okay?' Lisa said.

Henry was looking at the elaborate stitchwork in the carpet again.

'Look at me, pal,' she said gently. He made eye contact. 'You have to listen to Uncle Jack, no matter what. Okay?'

'Yes, Lisa.'

'Good. Enjoy yourself.' She smiled at him and ruffled his hair.

It would be the last time she saw him.

EIGHT

'And you've never heard from Henry again?' Harry asked.

Lisa shook her head. 'No. He and Jack both disappeared. I called the police and they tried to trace Jack's phone, but it was switched off. So was Henry's. He used it to take photos to send to me, usually of trains. But that time was different. There were trains in Stranraer, but they also went to the Galloway Wildlife Centre, near Barlae.'

'That's a wee bit down the road,' Liam said.

'Hardly a wee bit, Grandad.' Lisa looked back at Harry. 'It's close to ten miles.'

'Where was the phone last traced to?' Harry asked.

'Here. In Newton Stewart. Jack was going to take

Henry to see the ferries at the terminal in Cairnryan. There are no trains there, but Henry likes boats too. They were going trainspotting at Stranraer.'

'Isn't the ferry terminal at Stranraer?' Harry asked.

'Used to be until they moved it up the road,' Liam said. 'About ten years ago now.'

'Why didn't Jack just take Henry to Glasgow Central or Queen Street stations if he wanted to show him the trains?' Chloe asked.

'They'd done that. Edinburgh was on the cards, but Stranraer was down the road,' Lisa replied. 'It was really a couple of hours away, but Jack never did have a sense of time or direction. It was just a wee change of scenery, he said.'

'Why was he here?' Harry asked. 'There isn't a station here.'

'Jack sent me a text saying he was meeting up with a friend here. They were going to stay in a hotel overnight, then drive round to the centre. Which they did. They stayed at the hotel along the road. The Thistle. Henry sent me photos from the centre. Then they came here. Jack was meeting up with a friend of his. Archie. I don't know his second name. But he was a conspiracy nut, according to Jack. I didn't hear from them again.'

'What did Jack do for a living?' Chloe asked.

'He was a reporter. For the *Glasgow Mercury*. Trying to make his way into one of the red tops. Failing miserably.' Lisa was rubbing her hands together now as if there was an itch there. 'That's why we hired the private investigator. Davie Wylie.'

Harry perked up at that. 'What did he find out?'

'Nothing. We never heard from him again either. I mean, we thought he had skipped off with our money, but when I contacted his office, his secretary said he hadn't come back and she couldn't get hold of him.'

'Do you think he was a con artist?' Harry asked.

'No, definitely not,' Liam said, a little too loudly. 'It was a proper office in a serviced office building. He was also a former police detective. Davie Wylie. He used to be in Strathclyde. He seemed a solid bloke.'

'You went looking for him?' Harry asked.

'We drove down here to have a look for ourselves before we contacted Wylie. Jack sent Lisa a text telling her he was meeting a friend of her in an old house here. He gave her the address. This house was in bad shape. I mean, I've seen worse. Inside, it was cold and damp. But we found Henry's phone in there.' Liam pointed to the fireplace. 'In the ashes.'

'Did you give it to the police?' Chloe asked.

Lisa shook her head. 'What was the point? They didn't believe anything had happened to them.'

'What makes you say that?' Harry asked.

'Jack had written sensationalism pieces before. I think they thought this was just a stunt. Maybe something the paper had set up.'

'Then you contacted Davie Wylie?'

'Yes. He came here and looked around your house here, and then went to Barlae. Then we never heard from him again either.'

'I'd like to go and look at this wildlife centre,' Harry said.

'Good luck with that, son. Somebody torched it a couple of months ago. It's just a ruin now.'

They sat in silence for a moment, but for the crackling of the logs, which made it sound like the house was on fire. Then Harry got up.

'I'm going to make a phone call,' was all he said.

NINE

In the mudroom, Harry took out his mobile phone, the throwaway one, and dialled the number of a man he trusted more than anybody else in the world. When the call was answered on the other end, he felt relief.

'Jimmy? It's Harry.'

'Good to hear from you, Harry,' Dunbar said, genuine warmth in his voice.

'I need you to do a wee favour for me.'

'Since you're on official leave, I'm guessing it's police business.'

'You guess right. Do you think you could do me a solid?'

'No problem, Harry. Fire away.'

'I need a name run through the system, and a

licence plate,' Harry said, turning round to make sure nobody was listening to him.

'Wait till I grab a pen.' Harry waited for a few seconds before Dunbar came back on. 'Right, shoot.'

Harry gave him the details. 'I also want to ask if you know a copper called Davie Wylie. Ex-copper, I mean.'

'No, the name's not familiar to me. What's he done?'

'I'm talking to an old man and his granddaughter who hired him a year ago. Liam and Lisa McDonald. He went missing. He was looking for Lisa's ex, as he had gone missing with Lisa's younger brother. They've never been heard from since either. Any chance you could put the feelers out? See if you can find out anything about this Wylie bloke?'

'Aye, nae bother. Was Newton Stewart the last place they were known to be?'

'Sort of. The ex-husband, Jack, sent a text to Lisa saying he was meeting a friend in his house up a private road called Starry Hill Lane. It's my house, Jimmy. He told them he was here, stayed in a hotel overnight and went with a friend and the boy to the wildlife centre at a place called Barlae. Then he and the boy went missing. Then Lisa and her grandfather hired this Wylie guy, and he disappeared as well. Jack Easton is the ex's name.'

'Now that *is* a name I've heard of. He's a balloon who works for the *Mercury*. He's a sensationalist. Pain in the arse. I've seen him on TV, but not since he went missing, obviously. I remember something about that story in the news. As for Wylie, I haven't heard anything about him, but you know yourself, Harry, thousands of people go missing every year. Let me look into it more, though. I'll call you when I have something.'

'Thanks, pal.'

'Where are those folks now?'

'Inside my house. With my friend, Chloe.'

There was silence for a few moments. Broken by Harry again.

'Chloe Walker is my neighbour and drinking buddy, nothing else. We happen to live on the same wee road.'

'I didn't say a word, pal,' Dunbar answered.

'You didn't have to.'

'I'm not judging, son. It's your life. And life moves on. Have you been in touch with Jessica?'

Jessica was Alex's sister, back in Edinburgh, who was looking after Harry's daughter, Grace.

'I have. Everybody is doing fine.' *Doing fine*

without me.

'Right then. I'll call you tomorrow after I poke around a bit. Meantime, if you need me, just give me a call. And one more thing, Harry.'

'What's that?'

'Don't let the bastards grind you down.'

Harry smiled and hung up, going back into the house proper. The warmth of the fire felt good. The logs spat at him, like they weren't having a good time being burned. Bella perked up and barked at him until Lisa assured her it was only Harry. No axe, no murderous intentions and, sadly, no dog treats.

'My friend is going to look into it. He's a detective.'

'Thanks, Harry,' Lisa said. While her enthusiasm couldn't quite compete with a mariachi band, it had some warmth.

Chloe stood up. 'I'll get going. Nice meeting you all.'

'Likewise, hen,' Liam said.

'I'll walk down the hill with you,' Harry said.

'Aye, don't worry about us, son. We won't go raking about in your drawers while you're out,' Liam said.

'Nothing to find but pants and socks, Liam,' Harry said.

Harry and Chloe walked out into the rain, Chloe popping her umbrella up again. 'You'd better bring the one I lent you earlier,' she advised. 'Otherwise, all my umbrellas will be up here soon.'

Harry smiled, and after a few moments of searching, he found it, but held it by his side as Chloe put an arm through his and they walked back down the rutted road.

'You trust them, Harry?'

'Too late now if I don't. They could be pocketing my silverware as we speak, ready to do a runner.' He felt the rain pelt his left arm, the one holding the folded umbrella, as Chloe did her best to keep the other one over their heads. She wouldn't win any medals at it, but at least it wasn't inside out yet.

'No, I do trust them. I might not have had if it wasn't for wee Alice.'

'Maybe they just bring the wee girl along as a decoy.'

'Where did you learn to be so jaded, Chloe Walker?' The rain, the adrenaline from earlier and the coffee had sobered Harry up and he hoped Chloe couldn't feel his tension as she held his arm. Usually, they'd both had a drink and they threw caution to the wind.

'From having an ex-husband.'

'Ah. A story for another night?'

'Maybe I'll tell it to you tomorrow when we go and have a look for that wee boy.'

'What do you mean?' Harry stopped and his boot skidded on a couple of stones.

'They're here to look for family, and right now we're their best chance of help. The police aren't interested. They have nobody. They need us.'

'I suppose we could have a look around, but we have no authority.' *Well,* you *don't.*

'It won't do us any harm to talk to people. Since we're locals, they might open up to us.'

'We can only try.'

'Breakfast at your place? Nine o'clock?'

'Nine sounds fine.'

Chloe reached up and kissed him on the cheek, and he had a sudden flash of Alex's face, disapproving. 'You're a good man, Harry Mackay.'

She let go of his arm and walked away as he pressed the button for the umbrella to explode upwards and outwards in a futile attempt to keep him dry. Maybe one day he would tell Chloe his real name.

He waited until she was safely inside, but then a nagging question struck him: if it wasn't Lisa or Liam who had been in Chloe's house, who had it been?

TEN

'No sign of Calvin Stewart?' DS Robbie Evans said, bursting into the incident room like he had just scalded his bollocks with his coffee.

'I wish you wouldn't come in here like your arse hair's on fire,' Dunbar said. He was sitting in a huddle with DI Tom Barclay and DS Sylvia McGuire.

'I'm just raring to go this morning, boss.' Evans sipped the coffee and sat down on a chair. 'What have we got going on?'

'Glad you asked.' Dunbar stood up and grabbed his jacket from the back of his chair. He looked at Sylvia. 'Get onto that for me now, please, Sylvia. Call me.'

'Will do, sir.'

'Don't get comfortable,' Dunbar said to Evans.

'That's what she said.' Evans grinned.

'I'm not interested in what you and your old maw got up to last night.'

Evans dropped the grin. 'I meant...'

Too late, he had pulled a beamer and Sylvia was grinning along with Tom Barclay.

'Come on, let's go,' Dunbar said. 'We're going for a drive, so make sure you're wearing your disposable underpants if you're drinking that much coffee.'

'I'm a wee bit away from pissing the bed,' Evans retorted. 'Unlike you.'

'Shut your hole,' Dunbar replied as they made their way along the corridor.

'So where's the almighty DSup Calvin Stewart?' Evans asked.

'At Tulliallan. On a course or something. Maybe he got promoted to head canteen lady.'

'It's a bit quiet without him.'

'And to the Lord we thank it,' Dunbar said.

'Where are we going?' Evans asked.

'Loch Lomond.'

'Sweet. I fancied a day off.'

'Day off, ya hoor? This is no' the Boy Scouts you're in.'

'Been ages since I've been out of the city.'

'Carstairs hospital is outside the city. I can always make a phone call. I've always said you were certifiable anyway.'

'What are we going to Loch Lomond for?' Evans said in the car, trying to get the lid off his paper coffee cup without firing it all over his boss.

'A body on the shore at Luss. Pathologist is on the way, but it's suspicious. The guy has half his face missing, apparently.'

Evans splashed some of the hot liquid over his hand and onto the crotch of his trousers. 'Aw, bastard. Looks like I've pished myself now.'

'Why you drink that over-priced pish water is beyond me. Coffee with a name that sounds like a nob rash.'

'It's a young person's drink.'

'Snobby bastard's drink, more like.'

Evans shook his head. 'I hope this dries before we get there. Or maybe you could drive and I could take my trousers off and hold them up to the air vent.'

'Are you fuckin' daft? Somebody sees us in the car, you just in your Y-fronts, and I'd have to retire to the Outer Hebrides. If I see you so much as going near your fuckin' zip, I'll ram that coffee cup up your arsehole. Now get a bloody move on. Bloody dinosaurs went extinct faster than this. And were more intelligent.' Then a thought struck Dunbar. 'See that big T-rex fella? He had wee arms. Imagine him trying to hold a cup of coffee. He'd pour over it *his* baws as well.'

'Do you lie in bed at night thinking this pish up?' Evans wiped a hand over his front again. 'I hope this hasn't gone through to my skids.'

Dunbar shook his head and sat back for their drive.

'You know why I wear a tie to work, don't you?' he said.

'Because we're detectives and wearing a suit and tie is required.'

'No. So I can hang myself if the stress of listening to your pish gets too much.'

'Scooby would miss you, and the thought of no' spooning wi' your dug at night would make you think twice.'

'I'll spoon you in a minute, cheeky bastard.' Dunbar looked through the windscreen as they started their journey. 'That didn't sound right, though, did it?'

'It did not.' Evans grinned.

'You're twisting my melon, ya bastard. Maybe I'll just strangle you wi' my fuckin' tie.'

Dunbar closed his eyes and reclined the seat back a bit more as Evans took the Great Western Road and kept straight on when it became the A82.

'Did you watch...' Evans started to say. Dunbar started snoring. 'I know that's a fake snore.'

'It's a hint. Look in the mirror and tell yourself you're beautiful. Pretend you're in your bedroom.'

'Funny.' Although Evans did have a quick look, just to make sure no hair was out of place. Not that he gave the chat to women anymore, now that he had a girlfriend, Vern – and, he thought, it wouldn't matter if any hair was out of place if it still looked like he'd let his bladder go by the time they got to Luss.

'I'm drinking so much coffee because I'm knackered, in case you're interested,' Evans said.

'I'm not.'

'If I fall asleep and lose control and leave the road and only I survive, I'll tell them you took a benny and grabbed the wheel.'

'And if I survive as well, I'll put the steering wheel so far up your arse, you'll honk the horn every time you fart.'

A truck was in front of them and it slowed the car down. It was belching smoke, adding a small country's carbon footprint to the air all by itself.

'Turn right here,' Dunbar said.

'Where the signpost says *Luss*, you mean?' Evans made a face.

'Less of your bloody lip. Next time I see Muckle McInsh, I'll tell him to have Sparky use you as target practice.'

As Evans made the turn, a caravan-pulling bastard barrelled towards them, the approaching driver flashing his lights in either a *round you go, mate* way, or *what the fuck are you doing, moron?* way. Dunbar wasn't sure and didn't look round to see if the guy was wearing an anorak or a sleeveless pullover, but he was sure the man had stepped out of his *pulling my little house on wheels* comfort zone for a moment to tell Evans to fuck off. Before apologising to his wife.

Sorry, but that bounder pulled right in front of me.

That's quite alright, dear. But how do you know he's a count?

'The Loch Lomond Faerie Trail is along here, so you'll feel right at home,' Dunbar said, hoping the front of *his* trousers didn't look like he had pissed himself now.

'You would know about fairies,' Evans replied.

'I know. I just told *you*, didn't I?'

'You're the only one who thinks you're amusing.'

'Turn left opposite the hotel, then right at the chippie, I was told. It's a one-way, round in a circle,' Dunbar told him.

Evans slowed and took the street on the left at the end of the village. 'You ever been here before? Socially?' he asked Dunbar.

'Once. Cathy wanted to come here years ago. We had her mother with us. Her dad was working. It was a good day out. What about you?'

'Nope. Never been here. Never will be again.'

'Aye, if it's no' in a dark room with a disco ball spinning about to music that would stun a deaf man, then you're not interested. God forbid you should broaden your horizons.'

The street was narrow, necessitating the one-way system. The visitors' centre was on their left and the Luss parish church was on their right. A little lane ran down the side of the graveyard to the water, where the other police vehicles were waiting for them. Dunbar showed his warrant card to the uniform approaching them.

'The pathologist is waiting down there for you, sir,' he said, pointing vaguely in the direction of the loch.

They got out of the car, and although the sun

was out, it was weak and a chill wind swept in off the water.

'You mean where the forensics tent is pitched?' Dunbar said.

'Aye, that's it, sir.'

Dunbar couldn't figure out if the young man was taking the piss or not.

Over on the right was a boat shed.

'It's a boat rental place,' the uniform said, eager to please.

'Thanks, son,' Dunbar said, seeing traffic duty in the man's future.

They walked down towards a mini promenade that was really just a wide footpath skirting the loch. Uniforms were blocking the onlookers with blue-and-white police tape, like a marathon was about to break out.

'What's going on, luv?' an old woman with pink hair shouted to him. With her accent, she sounded like she could have been somebody's stunt double on *Coronation Street*.

Dunbar looked over at the forensics tent before looking back at the woman. 'Village fete,' he said. He was about to tell her not to go swimming with that hair colour. They didn't need another monster in a loch.

'You're a bad bastard, Jimmy Dunbar,' he said under his breath. But he didn't feel bad; the ghouls all wanted a glimpse of the dead man so they could fire it up onto social media.

'When I retire, if you ever see me in amongst a bunch of nosey-bastard tourists gawking at a crime scene, I give you permission to kick me in the bollocks,' he said to Evans.

'What about before you retire?'

'You'd be pissing into a wee bag taped to your leg for the rest of your life.'

'I was asking for a friend.'

The forensics tent looked like it was being held down by magic as the wind down by the shore of the loch was stronger. The scale went from *lightly ruffle your hair* to *blow your wig off* in a matter of feet. Luckily for the two detectives, neither of them kept their hair long enough to ruffle, never mind blow off.

'Christ, I like this place, but I'd rather sit in a pub and watch it through a window,' Dunbar said as they walked past more uniforms and into the tent itself, the pair of them snapping on nitrile gloves.

'Well, well, if it isn't Dr Who and her companion,' he said to the two women inside.

'It's the light that makes this thing look bigger inside,' said the older woman of the two. They were both dressed in white forensics suits. Dr Fiona Christie, Agatha to her friends. And her sidekick from the Glasgow City Mortuary whom Dunbar didn't recognise.

'This is our new assistant, Jackie Hyde.'

'How do?' he said. 'I'm DCS Jimmy Dunbar.' He looked back at Fiona.

'Does anybody call you Jekyll?' Evans asked.

'Not up until now.'

'He made me say it.'

'Nice to meet you both,' the young woman said, her eyes locking onto Evans.

Dunbar nudged him with an elbow. 'Tell the lassie your name.'

'Oh, aye, sorry. DS Robbie Evans.' They air-bumped fists like it was some kind of ritual that only they knew about.

Dunbar looked down at the figure on the concrete slipway of the boat launch. 'Come bobbing back up to the surface, did he?'

'No, he didn't.'

The man's facial features had been blown off with what everybody guessed was a shotgun. The crater that the birdshot had created was filled with dirt, and the blood and contents from his head had dried on the remainder of his face. His hands were almost skeletal, and dirty, just like the rest of him.

'A face only a mother could love,' Dunbar said. Then, to Fiona: 'Not in the water?'

'No,' Fiona said. 'He hasn't been in the water. There are no signs of bloating, which would have brought him to the surface if he'd been under. Somebody dumped him here.'

'Looks to me like he's been dead a while,' Evans said.

Dunbar looked at the younger detective as Evans looked over to Jackie, and he could tell Evans had been hoping to impress the woman. It was hard to tell if she was impressed or not, with her being suited up and looking like something that would chase Dr Who.

'That's very impressive, DS Evans.' This from Fiona. Jackie stayed tight-lipped. 'He has indeed. I'm no forensic anthropologist, but I would say he's been dead for about twelve to eighteen months. And I'd say he's been buried somewhere. Some of the dirt looks fresh.'

'Like he was just dug up?'

'Exactly. And there's too much dirt for it to mean he was in a coffin and then dug up. He looks like he's been in a shallow grave.'

'Any ID on him?'

'There was a wallet. Forensics have had a look and photographed it, but I asked them to leave the bag here for now until you saw it. You knew the guy. So did I.'

She picked up the bag from a corner of the tent like a magician might prepare his top hat with Bugs Bunny in it. Dunbar took it from her when it was obvious the pathologist wasn't going to spill the beans.

He took the wallet out and found a driving licence. 'Davie Wylie.'

Evans nodded slowly, knowing to keep his mouth shut. It was the man Harry McNeil had asked Dunbar about the night before.

Dunbar looked at Evans. 'Let's go for a walk.' Then, to the pathologist: 'Thanks, Fiona.'

'No problem. We'll get him loaded and transported down the road.'

Outside, they walked up the lane, Dunbar noticing the woman with the pink hair had gone. Probably given in to hypothermia and gone off for a nice cup of tea, or been put in a body bag. He stopped beside a sergeant.

'Has anybody searched around here?' he asked the uniform.

'No, sir. We were waiting for you.'

'Grab a couple of colleagues and we'll have a look around. Starting with this place.' Dunbar nodded to the gate set into the wall of the graveyard.

'Yes, sir.' The sergeant waved over a male and female officer and told them what he wanted.

'It couldn't be this easy, could it?' Evans said.

'Stranger things and all that.'

It turned out it could be that easy. The sergeant shouted to Dunbar from the back end of the church.

'Christ, I'll bet even that old woman with the hair heard that shout,' Dunbar said. Several heads turned in the direction of the church as Evans was last through the gate.

They caught sight of the sergeant, who had momentarily stepped out of view but was back now. He was waving again.

'I bet he was good at semaphore in the Scouts,' Dunbar said.

'Over here,' shouted a uniform, a young bloke who was obviously made from the same mould as the sergeant. Maybe they'd been watching an instructional video on how to shout and wave at a crime scene to attract the attention of the media.

They walked round the back of the church and saw what all the fuss was about. A grave had been dug open, and there was a young woman still in the hole.

'I think we found where he came from,' Dunbar said.

ELEVEN

Harry woke up to noises coming from another part of the house. Whilst he hadn't been drunk last night, the shots of vodka had certainly put him in the ballpark. He reached down for the baseball bat he kept under the bed, forgetting about his visitors for a moment.

Then he relaxed. Old Liam and the others.

He had chosen this room at the back of the house for his bedroom, and had an extension built out the back, just big enough to stick a bathroom in. The last thing he wanted was to climb the stairs when he was pished and fall, breaking a leg. He got up, showered, thought about shaving and decided the Queen wasn't coming today, and quickly got dressed.

Out in the living room, the logs were once again roaring in the grate.

Bella was the first to greet him, barking and growling for a second until she saw who it was, then she ran over, tail wagging. He petted her and she ran off again.

'Good morning,' Lisa said, smiling at him. 'Is there a laundromat in town?'

'No need. There's a laundry room off the mudroom. The machines are pretty straightforward.'

'Thanks. Grandad has to watch a YouTube video if he wants to wash his skids.'

'I heard that,' Liam said, coming in from the kitchen and putting a couple of plates down on the table at the back of the room. 'Breakfast coming right up, son. Full English or some toast?'

'Just some toast. I can get it.'

'Nonsense. Sit yourself down. I've made the coffees. Will your pal be joining us this morning?'

Harry looked puzzled for a moment, thinking the old man meant Jimmy Dunbar.

'Chloe,' Liam said, elaborating.

'Oh. No, I don't think so –' Harry started to say, and then, as if by magic, the front door opened and Chloe came in. Apparently, there was no need for an umbrella this morning. She smiled when she saw Harry.

'Good morning. Liam called and said he had the bacon on.'

How did he get your number? Harry thought he had sobered up pretty quickly, but obviously his detecting skills had got a bit rusty overnight.

'Bacon's on, hen,' Liam said, disappearing back through to the kitchen.

'You really did a good job with this place, Harry,' Lisa said.

'The builders took care of most of the work. I just painted it and I'm putting up some shelves.'

'He's a man of many talents,' Chloe confirmed.

Liam came back in with a couple of bacon rolls for Chloe and she sat down at Harry's table. The old man saw him looking.

'You still want toast? There's plenty of bacon left. And rolls.'

'Aye, go on then. You've twisted my arm.'

Liam scuttled away and came back a few minutes later with the rolls. Harry had to admit that the food tasted good, and he thought he should be grateful that the old man hadn't slit his throat while he was asleep.

After breakfast was done and the dog had been

fed and taken out for her morning constitutional, they sat on the couch and some chairs.

'We need to do a wee recap of last night, so it's fresh in our minds,' Harry said. 'Just a quick once-over.'

'Right,' Lisa said, quickly checking to see that Alice was amusing herself with her dolls away from the fire. 'Jack, my ex, took my brother to Stranraer, trainspotting, but I can't even be sure they actually went there. Henry didn't send me any photos from there. They went to the Galloway Wildlife Centre, and then Jack said he was meeting a friend here. They were going back to the centre again, after dark this time. We never heard from them again.'

'The police have done nothing this past year,' Liam said.

'Isn't it a bit dangerous to be staying overnight in the van?' Chloe asked.

Lisa looked at her grandfather before answering. 'We weren't just staying in it overnight. We live in it.'

Harry waited for the punchline, but none was forthcoming. 'Live in it?' he said.

'Aye, son, we live in it. I was living with Lisa, Henry and Alice. Lisa had to sell the house to pay Davie Wylie. I mean, not all of her money went to him, of course, but a good chunk of it. The rest we live on, with my pension.'

'Jesus, Liam, you can't have the bairn living out of a van,' Chloe said.

'We had no choice,' the old man said. 'We want Henry back. We've been looking for him.'

'And Jack?' Harry asked.

'Jack can burn in hell as far as I'm concerned,' Liam said. 'I never trusted him. An investigative reporter? I mean, how much does that pay?'

'He was always looking for the big one,' Lisa said. 'Convinced he was going to be the next Bob Woodward.'

'Was he working on a story when he went missing?' Harry asked.

'If he was, he didn't tell us. We came here after we heard about the centre burning down. Wylie's business partner told us,' Lisa said.

'It's the most proactive thing he's done since Davie went missing,' Liam added.

Harry nodded. 'I'll go down to the Thistle and ask Scramble if he knows anything. See if he can throw some light on things,' he said.

'I'll come with you,' Liam said.

'No. You stay here with Lisa. Keep the doors locked.'

'I'll come with you,' Chloe said. 'I've lived here a while now and they know me better than they know you.'

Harry didn't quite see the logic. If people didn't want to talk, it didn't matter how long you had lived in a place. 'If I protest, will it do any good?'

Chloe smiled. 'I'll just use your facilities and then we'll get off.'

TWELVE

Harry checked his phone again, scrolling through the photos that Lisa had sent him from her own phone. One of her ex, Jack Easton, and another of Henry, her brother, and the friend, Archie.

Chloe drove a little nondescript hatchback that went a lot faster than the impression it gave when it was sitting in her driveway. Harry was a nervous passenger, something he tried not to show to people. Luckily, the first part of the journey was two minutes from their private road, a quick test of the waters regarding Chloe's ability to cope with moving her vehicle when there were other vehicles on the road. Or when she was sober.

'If you're going to drive me about, I want to make

sure you have enough petrol,' Harry said. 'You can fill up in here.' He pointed to the petrol station.

'You might not have noticed how quiet the car is, but this is electric, Harry.'

He looked at her, grinning from behind the steering wheel.

'I knew that.'

'Nobody loves a smart arse, eh?' she said, the smile still on her face.

Harry held up his hands. 'I'm saying nothing.'

'However, I will pull in and use their wee shop. I want a drink for us to take on the road.'

'You know we're only going round to Barlae.'

'What if we break down somewhere on the way? We could be stranded for days. They say you should be prepared for anything.'

'I hardly think we're going to be wiped out by a tornado, and the snow is months away.'

'You were never in the Boy Scouts, I can tell.' She laughed as she pulled into the side of the petrol station, near a big sign that said, *No parking – staff only*.

'Here are the keys,' she said, getting out and fishing the keys out for him. 'Just in case somebody moves you along.'

He thought his warrant card might do the trick if push came to shove but took her keys anyway.

'You want anything?' she asked.

'Pint of lager and a packet of pork scratchings, please.'

'Sorry, we're not in the pub yet.'

'Bottle of water? Here, take the money.'

'No, you supplied breakfast. I'll get it.' She closed the door and he watched her walk into the petrol station. He was amazed again by how much she looked like Alex from behind. Was that why he got on so well with her? His friend and neighbour looked exactly like his dead wife?

He took his mobile phone out and punched in a number.

'Jessica? It's Harry.'

'Hi, Harry!' Alex's sister was always pleased to hear from him. He wondered if he would be the same if the shoe was on the other foot, if she'd skipped off and left her baby daughter with him to look after. Jessica was obviously built of sterner stuff than he was.

'How's Grace?'

'She's doing fine. Everything's okay.'

'The nursery okay?'

'Yes, the business is fine. As you can hear.'

Harry heard the sound of kids in the background. He had been left the nursery by a former girlfriend of his in her will.

'I appreciate what you're doing, Jessica.' It sounded lame, even to him.

'I encouraged you, didn't I? I'm on your side, Harry. Frank Miller popped round to see how you were. He doesn't have your number.'

'Only you have this number,' he said, a little more aggressively than he'd wanted.

'I won't give anybody your number, don't worry.'

'I'm not suggesting you would. Frank means well.'

'He does.' There was a pause for a moment before she carried on. *'The lawyers said they're ready to list your flat when you give them the go-ahead.'*

'I will. Soon.'

The flat that he had shared with Alex. Where she had collapsed. He knew he should sell it as soon as possible, but he was holding back for some reason. He had lived there when he had been seeing Vanessa, the girlfriend who had left him everything in her will. She had left him a big house in Murrayfield, near the nursery, as well as a large sum of money. She'd had nobody else to leave it to, and this still made him feel guilty. He wondered if she had done this because she had thought they would be getting married one day? Of course, he had fallen out with her and had got together with Alex, and Vanessa had either been very forgiving or hadn't got around to changing her will. Either way, he knew he was comfortable financially.

'I'll call you later in the week, Jessica. Tell Grace I love her.'

'Okey-dokey.' She cut the call, and Harry sat looking out of the passenger window. Did he love Grace? Of course he did. Then why was he running away from her? Running away from his former life?

He didn't have the answer.

The force psychologist, Harvey Levitt, had a penchant for telling it how it was. He wasn't there to mollycoddle but to help somebody onto the right track. Harry had sat and discussed his imminent departure down to the south of Scotland with Levitt. The big man hadn't tried to discourage him but had guided him.

'If it's something you have to do, Harry, then do it. Just make sure the little one doesn't suffer because of it,' Levitt had said.

But Harry had had all his ducks in a row before pulling the trigger on his move. He had told Jessica that he had bought a wee place to do up, to take his mind off things.

She had agreed to look after Grace. Plus, she had lost her job and the nursery needed a new manager, and since Jessica had a business degree, she took over the running of the nursery.

And took over the parental role for Grace.

Otherwise Harry would have put her up for adoption.

Just the thought of doing that made him feel icy cold inside. Alex would have killed him before she'd have let him do that, but if she had still been here, then there would have been no need to put her up. And that was the problem he had and it was driving him crazy.

Chloe came back and got in behind the wheel.

'Everything okay?' she asked. 'You look like you lost a pound and found a penny.'

'Oh, I was just thinking about a friend of mine. No longer with us.'

'Oh, sorry.'

'Don't be.' He handed her back the keys and she moved the car a little way along the road, then parked outside the auction mart, opposite the hotel.

'No problems at the house last night?' he asked her as the quiet car became even quieter.

'No. I was thinking of reporting it after we leave here.'

'It wouldn't do any harm.' Except it wasn't just a housebreaker. Or a transient thief, like Harry had accused old Liam of being. Somebody had been in the house for a purpose and it wasn't to take the TV.

They got out, the air smelling damp from the rain overnight. The roads and pavements were still wet, like it was only a reprieve. They crossed to the hotel's reception door, along from the entrance to the bar.

Inside, a young girl with a smile who was new and not yet jaded was behind the desk.

'Good morning. Can I help you?'

'I'm Harry Mackay and this is Chloe Walker. We're friends of Scramble's. Could you see if he's available?'

'Of course. Give me one second.' She picked up the handset and Harry turned away. Chloe did the same.

'What's Scramble's real name?' he asked her.

'I have absolutely no idea. I've always called him by that name. I never thought to ask.'

'He'll be along shortly,' said the girl at the desk. 'If you want to take a seat, you can wait there for him.'

'Thank you,' Harry said, turning to look at her. They sat on a couch behind a table.

'I don't think I've ever been in this part,' Chloe said.

'Do you go drinking in any of the other bars in town?'

'No, just here. Because it's down the road. I mean, I don't drink and drive; I just take a taxi. It doesn't cost much and saves me walking up that road of ours. What about you?'

'Since I came here, I've had a pint in a couple of bars, but I like the Thistle because it's nearer.'

A figure approached from behind the reception desk. 'Well, well, you two must love this place. You can't keep away!' Scramble said.

They both stood up and approached the big man.

'We just wanted a word, Scramble, if you could spare us a few minutes,' said Harry.

'For my two best customers, of course. Come away down to the bar and we'll have a coffee.'

'Thanks,' Chloe said.

'Well, if it wasn't for you two coming in here and getting drunk every night, I'd have to lay off staff.'

'We just like keeping the local economy going,' Harry said.

'Don't let me stop you, my friend,' Scramble said.

They went into the bar and Scramble asked the barman to bring them three coffees and they sat at a table.

'Now, what do you need my help with?'

Harry brought his phone out. 'This man went missing about a year ago, with his brother-in-law and a friend. Three of them vanished.' He showed Scramble the photo. 'A friend of mine is in town looking for him again. She asked if I wouldn't mind helping. She knew I'd moved here now, so she asked for help.'

The big man looked at the photo on the phone. 'I remember him. It was on the news. He stayed here. The police came here one time and asked about him, but I couldn't tell them anything. Well, not much anyway. All I could tell them was, he was here to visit the centre with the boy, and he was meeting with a friend of his. Archie Spencer. A local lad.'

'Did you know this Archie guy?'

'Aye. Archie is well-known around here. He's a conspiracy nut. Thinks that aliens are hiding in the woods and that everything from the Twin Towers to the D-Day landings was a hoax. He's a loner. But he also thought the government covered up any UFO sightings. Before he went missing, he lived with his old maw. I'm surprised to learn he had any friends.'

'Did he work?'

'He was a caretaker at the church. That was his official line to people, but I'm sure the minister felt sorry for him and let him into the church to sweep up and change light bulbs, that sort of thing.'

'Do you know if his mother still lives here?' Harry asked him.

'Aye. I see her in Sainsbury's along the road. She never seemed to get over Archie going missing. You know, there was a guy who came here shortly afterwards and started asking questions. He said he was a private investigator. I told him the same thing I'm telling you: this Jack bloke was going to the centre with Archie the next day.'

'The next day?' Chloe asked.

'Aye. Jack was in the bar that night. Archie came in and they had a drink. I asked Jack about the boy and he said he was in the room watching movies on his iPad. He was safe enough up there. Archie and Jack sat in a corner, whispering and drawing stuff on a pad. I heard them say they were going to the Galloway Wildlife Centre the next day after dark.'

'Jack checked out with the boy?' Harry asked.

'He did that. I never saw him again. It was the

talk of the town for a while. Some say Archie got his wish and was taken aboard the mothership.'

'And what do you say, Scramble?' Harry asked.

'My honest opinion? I think Jack took the boy to get back at his ex-wife. I think Archie helped him. Maybe they all moved down to the south of England. That's what I think.'

'The minister who runs the church, will he be in the church today?'

'If he's not off doing his rounds. He's a very busy man.'

They stood up and Harry thanked Scramble. 'No doubt we'll see you in the bar tonight.'

Scramble grinned. 'I've got to keep my staff in a job.'

THIRTEEN

Jimmy Dunbar called his DI, Tom Barclay, and asked him to bring a team up to Luss. He could be in charge of the investigation up here. Dunbar suspected in his gut that Davie Wylie had been buried up in the graveyard but not murdered there. Wylie wouldn't have let himself be taken all that way just to have his face blown off. And who was the girl? He didn't think anything would come from a door-to-door, but you never knew. Maybe somebody would remember something from a year ago. Some strange light in a graveyard in the middle of the night. Somebody out walking a dog spotting a strange car parked on the driveway.

They were heading back down to Glasgow. He had called DS Sylvia McGuire, who said she would get an address for where Wylie last worked and lived. And yes, she would call Harry McNeil when all the requested checks came back, which shouldn't be too long.

'I've never seen the attraction of pulling a caravan, have you?' Evans said.

'I've been to a static caravan for a week's holiday with Cathy's old man. At least that's the size of a house. Those fucking things you tow that sway about on the motorway are coffins on wheels. In order to drive one, you have to get your wife to cut your hair, wear extra-thick glasses, tuck your shirt into your underwear and have a pet Yorkie. Maybe pour coffee on yourself to look like you've pished yourself.'

'It's too much like hard work,' Evans replied, ignoring the jibe about spilling coffee on himself. 'Having to load the thing up, then be twice as careful when you're driving. Not to mention keep looking in the rear-view mirror to make sure the fucking thing's still following you. Naw, that's not for me.'

'Bit of a lazy bastard, aren't you? You only get out of life what you put into it. Like that guy who flashed his lights at you is feeling quite proud of himself that he almost cut us in half.'

Evans looked at him and made a face. 'What are

you talking about? That was a flash to let me cross over.'

'Bollocks. We almost had to be cut out of the car.'

'Are you like this when Cathy drives you about?'

'I wouldn't dare, son.'

Dunbar took his phone out and made a call. 'Muckle, ya hoor,' he said by way of a greeting. 'How's life treating you, son?'

'Not so bad, boss. How's things yourself?'

'Ah, you know how it is: another day, another episode of nearly shiting myself with Heid the baw driving. Nothing new.'

Muckle laughed. *'That laddie's going to get a complex.'*

'I'll make a man of him, don't you worry.' Dunbar looked quickly at Evans to make sure the younger sergeant got the message. Evans mouthed words that wouldn't have been appropriate in front of his granny.

'The reason I'm calling is, I want to ask if you know somebody. Davie Wylie. He was one of us, then went private, like you.'

'Davie? Aye, we knew him. I haven't seen him for a long time. He didn't reply to my last call, many moons ago.'

'That's because he's been dead. About a year now.'

'Jesus. How?'

'I'd rather talk face to face. You spare us a minute?'

'I can spare you more than that. Vern and I are in the office. Shug's here too.'

'We're a wee bit out. We were at Loch Lomond.'

'We'll be here, boss.'

'I have to go to Wylie's office first, then we'll be round.'

Dunbar disconnected the call and looked at Evans. 'After Wylie's office, we'll go and see Muckle McInsh. Vern's there, and I swear to God, if you start blubbering and foaming at the mouth, your bollocks will have an appointment with my steel toe cap. Now, don't spare the horses, and avoid caravans for fuck's sake.'

Robbie Evans grinned and planted his foot on the gas pedal.

FOURTEEN

Harry realised that he hadn't really got to know Chloe. Yes, they were neighbours on their wee private road, and they said hello in passing then they would have a drink at night in the bar, but for the first couple of months, he had been so self-absorbed after losing his wife that he had retreated into his shell, only coming out when it was time to get drunk.

'I'm glad you didn't object to me coming along with you today, Harry,' Chloe said, driving along Arthur Street.

'I'm too tired to argue.'

'I know you've only been in your house for a few months, and we don't invite each other over for tea, but I want to get to know you better. As a friend.'

'I like walks on the beach, watching the sunset –

and animals. I volunteer at the old folks' home and enjoy a sociable drink with friends.'

'We don't have a beach, we do have a sunset, I'm sure you like animals. Not sure you're not telling porkies about the old folks' home, and yes, you do enjoy a sociable drink with friends. As dating site profiles go, I'd think you were a closet serial killer.'

A slight smile played across his lips as she approached the police station. *I've met some serial killers and trust me, that wouldn't be their profile on a dating site.*

Chloe pulled into the side of the road, into a little layby with *No Turning* painted on the tarmac, the letters now faded.

The front door was facing them. Harry got out into the chilly air and stretched his arms. 'What do you reckon the chances are of my house not being tanned while we're out?' he said.

'Not high. Sometimes you have to take a leap of faith in life, Harry.'

They walked up the short ramp and into the police station. There was a sergeant behind the front desk.

'Help you?' he asked.

'I'd like to report somebody being in my house last night,' Chloe said.

'A housebreaking?'

'Not exactly. He got in through a window that wasn't locked.'

'Did he steal anything?'

'Not that I can see,' Chloe said.

'So, he didn't break his way into your house, and he didn't steal anything. What is it you're trying to report?' He was a man who looked to be in his forties, who was paddling along in the force until one day he could hang up his uniform for good.

'Oh. It does seem a bit trivial when you put it like that. Sorry to have bothered you.' She turned away from the counter, expecting Harry to follow, but Harry walked up closer.

'Who's in charge of this station?'

'Inspector Robertson. Why?'

Harry turned to look at Chloe, who was looking out through the glass in the door. 'I'd like to speak with him about an incident.'

'Your house get broken into too, did it?'

Harry got in the man's face. 'Tell him I want a word. Go and make it happen.'

The man was about to object when another man in a white shirt walked into the back area. 'What's all the noise?'

'I need to have a word with the man in charge,' Harry said. 'It's about the missing people.'

A look passed between the inspector and the sergeant, and the inspector was the first to speak. 'Come on through.'

'The lady still needs a report taken,' Harry said.

'I can do that right now,' said the sergeant.

'I won't be long,' Harry said to Chloe as she turned back to look at him. The sergeant buzzed him through to the back and Harry went through the door the inspector had disappeared through a minute ago. There were more uniforms through here and a couple of civilians sitting at a desk.

'What's this information you have?' The inspector seemed sceptical and only perked up when Harry showed him his warrant card. 'DCI Harry McNeil.'

'You should have said, sir.' The inspector picked up his phone and called through to the front desk, telling the sergeant there to pull his finger out of his arse before slamming the phone down.

'I appreciate that.' Harry took his phone out and opened the photos app. 'This young man and the teenager went missing about a year ago. Along with one of your locals. Were you here when it happened?' He showed the photo of Jack Easton, then swiped, showing Henry. He didn't have a photo of Archie Spencer but gave Robertson the name anyway.

'I was here. We had everybody out looking for them and drafted in reinforcements. There was no sign of them. Nothing.' He looked at Harry. 'Nobody knows you're a police officer.'

'I'd like to keep it that way. I'm on a leave of absence right now.'

'As you wish, sir.'

'Who led the investigation?' Harry asked.

'I don't want to talk ill of anybody. You know how word gets around.'

'Listen, I want you to keep my identity under wraps just now. What you tell me is in confidence.'

Robertson sat back for a moment, a worried look fleetingly touching his face.

'I literally have six months until I retire. I do not want to rock any boats. I hope you understand that sir?'

'I do. What's your first name, Inspector?'

'Mike.'

'Well, Mike, I can assure you that the conversation we're having is between you and me.'

'Sometimes I hate this job. I wanted to be a

career copper, and I achieved that, but at some expense.'

'What do you mean?' Harry asked.

'I was based in Glasgow. I cocked up. Made a wee mistake, and then I was sent here, put out to pasture. Then, when that missing persons' case hit my desk, I saw it as a way to redeem myself. Archie Spencer went missing too, as you said. He lives here. I spoke to his mother and the vicar at the church. Wall of silence doesn't even begin to describe it.

'Then, suddenly, I get a call from a superintendent in Glasgow. Big mouthy bastard. Sorry, I don't mean to disrespect senior officers, but he came down on me like a ton of bricks. Shouting on the phone, telling me to keep my nose out of an investigation. It was being handled by Glasgow, and if they needed my help, they wouldn't ask for it. Basically, I was warned off, and the threat of losing my pension was too great to make me fight them.'

'I don't understand why that would happen. Just because you were looking into the disappearance of a young man?'

'No, sir. It's because of who that young man is. Everybody round here thinks he's the village idiot, but he's almost like Batman: what you see normally is just a charade. I had spoken to somebody who knew Archie. The guy is a computer genius, and friends with Jack Easton. Have you investigated Easton's background? He is, or was, whatever his status is now, an investigative reporter. Archie is a conspiracy nut, but he's also a great believer in UFOs. From what his mother told me, he used to go up to the Galloway Wildlife Centre. He went there often. Then one day, he got excited about something. He gave Jack Easton a call. Next thing his mother knew, Jack was here with a teenage boy. The three of them were seen around town, and up at the centre. They were here one night, and Archie's mother said they were planning to go back to the centre, but the next night, when it was dark. She never heard from him again.'

'A private detective came down from Glasgow looking around, I heard.'

Robertson nodded. 'Davie Wylie. I knew him, way back. Good bloke.'

'And you haven't heard anything about him again?' Harry asked.

'No, nothing.' Robertson leaned forward. 'The desk sergeant is a wee sweetie wife. It wouldn't surprise me if your name is all over the town by tonight. If you want my advice, sir, watch your back. Glasgow doesn't like people sticking their nose in.'

'It seems strange that Glasgow would have so much influence over a small Ayrshire town.'

'It's because of the estate,' Robertson said.

'Estate?'

'The Corcoran estate. In the middle of bloody nowhere, but it seems the town was built around it. Maybe hundreds of years ago, it was a quiet hunting place or whatever. Now it's still in the same family, but they have a reach beyond anything you can imagine. They're Teflon: nothing sticks.'

'Where is this estate?'

Robertson laughed, but there was no humour. 'Don't even think about going there, sir. The Corcoran family are powerful and they have a lot of powerful friends. As you will see very soon, if you go to Barlae. The special guests are already arriving for the Autumn Bonanza.'

'What's that?'

Robertson thought about it for a moment. 'Have you ever heard of Bohemian Grove in California?'

'I don't think I have.'

'It's a private estate, and the rich and powerful go there to a camp once a year, I think. And when I say famous, I mean famous. I think even the Queen has been. Presidents, actors, all sorts. Nobody talks of it, but there are rumours of what they get up to. You can read about it online. Well, the Corcoran estate is moulded in the same way. Politicians come here, actors, all sorts of rich people. They have this big meeting once a year, and Archie, being the conspiracy theorist that he is, went into overload round about now. But last year, he was especially pumped up about something, his mother said. He wouldn't talk about it, but he'd found something out. And he wanted to share it with his friend Jack Easton.'

'And somebody from Glasgow jumped all over you?'

'Chief Inspector Willie Munroe. Absolute twat. The estate hires private security, but the police direct traffic and things like that.'

'Archie worked in a church?' Harry asked.

'Yes, he did. His mother said he wasn't living in her house rent free. So I think he got the job that took up the least amount of his time. And one where he would last more than five minutes.'

'I'd like to go and talk to Archie's mother. Does she work?'

'She owns a guest house. She was busy when I was talking to her about her son. I'll give you her address.' Robertson took out a piece of paper and jotted it down.

'What about the minister? Can I contact him?'

'The church is round the corner. Turn right out of here, then right again. The church is up on the right-hand side. The minister's house is in the grounds. Reverend Baxter.'

Harry stood up and shook the man's hand. 'Thanks for seeing me. I drink in the Thistle every night if you're ever in there.'

'I sometimes go in there.'

'One more thing. My friend Chloe is reporting somebody being in her house last night. The sergeant wasn't taking her seriously. He didn't break in, whoever it was, and he didn't take anything, but there were muddy boot-prints left behind. Somebody was in there having a look around.'

'I'll make sure patrols are going past there regularly.' Robertson lifted the phone and spoke into it before hanging up.

'Thanks. If you come in the pub, a few beers are on me.'

Harry left the office and went looking for Chloe. He found her waiting for him in the waiting room.

'Suddenly, he was very charming,' she said as they made their way back to her car. The clouds had come in, making a chilly day that little bit colder.

'Archie Spencer worked in the church round the corner. I want to go and talk to the minister.'

'Show me the way.'

Chloe did a turn in the road, despite the warning from the faded yellow letters.

'How did you get on?' Harry asked her.

'He took the report. Whatever it was you said to that inspector worked.'

'Turn right here.'

She turned and quickly looked at him. 'What *did* you say to him?'

'Not much really. Just a little trick I picked up a long time ago.'

FIFTEEN

Robbie Evans pulled up outside of what had once been a Georgian townhouse but was now offices.

'Can you imagine living in here, back in the day?' he said to Dunbar, who had taken his phone out.

'Not really.'

'I can. I think I was born in the wrong century. What year do you reckon this was built?'

'Robbie, how the bloody hell should I know when it was built? Do I look that old to you?'

Evans opened his mouth to answer, but the look Dunbar gave him snapped his mouth shut.

They were in the south side of Glasgow now, having made it back without encountering any more rogue caravans.

Dunbar took his phone out and made a call. 'Sylvia, it's me, DCI Dunbar.'

'Hello, sir.'

'Any results yet?'

'I was reading some reports from the Jack Easton slash Henry McDonald disappearance. If you ask my opinion, the bigwig from Glasgow swept it under the carpet. It died a sudden death.'

'What's his name?'

'Chief Inspector Willie Munroe.'

'Do me a favour, find out all the details you can on him. On the QT. If for some reason it comes back on you, I'll deal with him. Meantime, Robbie and I are at Davie Wylie's office. We got back here in one piece, yes. Talk to you later.' He hung up.

'One piece? May I remind you who it was who saved your life when that out-of-control caravan driver put the welly down? My sharp eyes and even sharper reflexes prevented you from near-certain death.'

'You said earlier the bastard was flashing you to cross. Make up your fucking mind.'

'Aye well, I'm just saying. If that was the case, then I saved your life.'

'You don't half talk some pish, Robbie. I might have

to call your mother and tell her to stop letting you drink that fake orange juice pish. You know, the stuff they sell to kids that's only association with orange is the colour.'

'I don't drink that stuff.'

'Maybe stop putting vodka on your cornflakes in the morning then.' Dunbar got out and stepped onto the pavement. *This would have made quite the gaff right enough,* he thought.

'There are a few offices in here. Third floor is where Davie worked,' Dunbar said.

They walked into a carpeted hallway, with white stone pillars and a staircase facing them, and they carried on up to the third floor and saw a sign on one of the doors: *Wylie & Chalmers, Private Investigators.* Dunbar felt his legs starting to ache slightly, or more to the point, his knees. Now he wished the exercise bike had won the toss-up last Christmas instead of the foosball table.

He opened the door and walked in with Evans behind. A woman sat behind a desk, tapping away at a keyboard, her head bobbing up and down as she alternated between the keys and looking at the screen to check her typing.

'Can I help you?' she asked after a couple of minutes. Dunbar thought a man with an axe wouldn't have any worries about using stealth if he decided to pay them a visit at the office.

'DCI Dunbar,' he said, showing his warrant card and then introducing Evans. 'I'd like to speak with Mr Chalmers. I called ahead.'

The room was a fair size, with a couple of chairs over by the window. A door was off to the left of the desk.

'Ah, yes. The great DCI Dunbar.'

'I'm sorry?'

'His words, not mine. Chubby Chalmers. Like Chubby Checker, without the talent. Or the money.'

The door opened and a large man came barrelling out towards them.

'Ho-ho, now, now, Agnes, what have I told you about gossiping?'

'You told me to go ahead and gossip as much as I liked as long as I could type.'

'Well, at least you're an expert at one of them.' He stepped forward and held out a hand. 'Ross Chalmers.'

Chubby, Agnes mouthed behind his back.

'DCI Dunbar. DS Evans. Can we talk privately?'

'Aye, of course. Agnes, could you make us some coffee?'

'Yes, Mr Chalmers, sir.' She got up from behind her desk, made a face and did a little curtsy.

They walked through the door into a short hallway. On the right was a sink with a kettle and some mugs on it. Underneath was a fridge. There were no windows in here and a weak light shone above the cups. Dunbar looked at one of the mugs, turned to Evans and nodded in the direction of the offending vessel. Evans screwed up his face. Dunbar thought there was a better than fifty per cent chance of getting typhoid off a mug, so he declined the offer. Evans, likewise.

'Suit yourselves,' Agnes said, retreating. 'Coffee tastes like pish anyway,' she mumbled almost under her breath as she closed the door into the reception area.

Chalmers' office was the type of mess a bull could only dream of aspiring to in a china shop. If you were being charitable, you would offer the loan of a can of petrol and a box of matches. Papers were scattered over the top of the desk, and Dunbar spotted a half-eaten doughnut with jam oozing out of the middle.

The office itself was quite large, with a view of a garden below and a similar building opposite.

'I told the bloody cleaner not to fanny about with

my papers. Go round them, I said, but oh no, she scatters stuff like she's pished when she's cleaning. You wouldn't believe the amount of tidying up I have to do every morning.'

'A wee bit delayed this morning?' Dunbar asked.

'What? Oh, aye. Just grab those box files off the seats there and grab a pew.' Chalmers managed to clear enough space so the plate holding his doughnut could get its own real estate.

'I only ate half because I'm on a diet,' he lied.

Dunbar thought the only way the man could lose weight was if he trimmed his nose hairs. He watched as Evans lifted a couple of box files, and Dunbar was tempted to tell his colleague to throw them out the window, but he nodded vaguely in the direction of a piece of carpet that was poking through the clutter, and Evans deposited them there. Dunbar lifted the one on his side and casually tossed it onto another pile of paper. He checked for any errant blobs of jam that might have come firing out of the doughnut before sitting down. He would hate to have to ram the half-eaten piece of dough down the fat man's throat.

'Agnes mentioned Davie Wylie. What do you want to know about him?'

'Who murdered him,' Dunbar said. He noticed

Chalmers had already forgotten about the mythical diet he was on and had lifted the doughnut halfway to his lips before pausing.

'Davie's dead?'

He put the doughnut back down onto the plate and put that back onto the desk.

'People usually are after they've been murdered. What can you tell me about the missing persons' case he was working on when he went missing a year ago?'

Chalmers licked his fingers without missing a beat, and wiped them on something out of sight, probably his trousers. Suddenly, Evans spilling coffee down his crotch didn't seem so bad.

'I looked up the files while you were on your way here. A woman's ex-husband and her brother had gone down to Stranraer trainspotting. They then went to the Galloway Wildlife Centre and then they were meeting with a friend of the ex's, somebody called –' he flipped open a buff folder – 'Archie Spencer. They went on their way the following day and then disappeared.'

'Is there anything in your notes to suggest that Wylie made any headway?' Dunbar asked.

Chalmers shook his head. 'Dead, eh? Now I wish I hadn't called him a no-good thieving bastard.'

'Why would you call him that?' Evans asked.

'He skipped off with the money that lassie had paid him. I mean, the money goes into the business. It's not as if we keep it for ourselves. But no, he was off with the money.'

'Anything in the notes?' Dunbar asked again.

'Oh. Hang on.' Chalmers opened the file and patted his head with one hand, indicating that he was either daft or he usually kept a pair of reading glasses up there. 'Have you seen my glasses?'

'What do they look like?' Evans said.

'Well...like glasses. Only they're for reading with.'

'I meant...' Evans started to say, but Dunbar shook his head. *Ignore the fat bastard.*

'They're around here someplace. Bastard things. I need one of those string things people wear round their neck so they don't lose their glasses. I had one ages ago, but I lost it.'

Chalmers opened first one desk drawer, then another. 'Ah, here they are. How the hell did they get in there?'

Dunbar's boot was getting antsy, as if it had sensed there was an arse to be stuck up.

'Is there anything in the file, Mr Chalmers?' he asked.

Chalmers put his glasses on, perching them on the end of his nose, and made a face to keep them there as he perused the paperwork inside the file. He mumbled as he read. Dunbar put an elbow on the arm of his chair and rubbed the bridge of his nose, picturing shooting Chalmers.

'Nope. Fuc– I mean, nothing there.' Chalmers took his glasses off and leaned in closer. 'Agnes doesn't like it when I swear. She's in another room and can still hear when I'm on the phone swearing. I think she's got some sort of special powers. Maybe a witch in another life and couldn't quite let it go. Know what I mean?'

'And you were going to let her make us coffee?' Dunbar said.

'Well…you and him coffee. Not me. I go to Starbucks. I wouldn't trust her as far as I could spit coffee at her. But alas, gentlemen, there's very little to go on regarding Davie.'

'You don't seem very cut up about it, if you don't mind me saying,' Dunbar said, not giving a monkey's baw bag whether the man minded or not.

'I didn't like him, truth be told. I knew he was an ex-cop, and he was advertising for a partner, and I talked with him and decided to invest. He talked a good game but turned out to be an arsehole. God rest his soul. He was always on the phone, whispering and the like.'

'Where was his office?' Evans asked. 'There's only one desk in here.'

'There's a smaller office next door. Broom cupboard more like. Although a broom would go on strike if it knew it had to live in there. I thought it would do for a wee while. He said we were moving soon. That was my office. The men building the Burma railway had better working conditions. When he didn't come back, I took his office.' Chalmers swept an arm around. 'And that's basically where we are now. Davie was alright, don't get me wrong, but I wouldn't name my firstborn after him. After I started here, I soon realised he was shifty, and that's putting it mildly.'

Sweat had broken out on his forehead, like a Roman army appearing on the horizon. Or maybe the impending heart attack that was always only one doughnut away had come knocking.

'What do you mean, *shifty?*' Dunbar asked, feeling the room getting stuffy, as if the big man was pumping out more heat than the radiator behind him.

Chalmers held out his hands. 'You know, shifty. Dodgy.'

'I'm up on the definition of shifty and dodgy,' Dunbar replied, making it sound like he was talking about the resident musicians in a working men's club.

'I mean, taking phone calls and lowering his voice when I approached, then going in the opposite direction and shouting in here with the door closed, like an exorcism was taking place and he was spitting at the priest. That sort of thing. Not sharing anything with me. It was like I had been interviewed by one man, and the twin had come to work wearing the same sweater. It didn't help his case that he was ginger too. You know what those mad bastards are like. So if you're asking, did I murder him? The answer is no. Would I have liked to? Yes. Would it have come to that point if he'd still been working here? Most definitely. But alas, he pissed off somebody else obviously, which doesn't surprise me. Davie Wylie was a walking disaster. I can only imagine how he was as a copper. And you know what those bast—'

Chalmers stopped suddenly, his brain flashing a red light, reminding him that the pair of bastards sitting opposite him were in the same club that Davie Wylie had been a member of.

'Do you know of anybody who would want to kill Wylie?' Evans asked.

'Take your pick. It could have been somebody he had put behind bars a long time ago, or it could be connected to the missing people he was looking for. Considering that's when he went missing, I'd go with option two. But I can only go by the file on these people. I didn't talk to them, didn't meet them, so I don't know if they're members of a band of gypsies or part of a cult. He never discussed anything with me. He wanted the exciting cases I think, leaving the bread-and-butter stuff for me. You know, cheating husbands. Cheating wives too, but it's mostly husbands. Boring stuff, but it suits me. I sit in a car with a camera and try to take photos of them with their trousers down. Failing that, at least with the younger piece on their arm, and it's invariably younger women they go with.'

'Did anybody ever call here looking for Mr Wylie?' Evans said, still showing respect to an older detective of senior rank, even though he hadn't known Wylie personally.

'Nobody. Oh, wait – there were a couple of calls afterwards, but they were hang-ups. I didn't think anything of it at the time, because that happens a lot. Somebody wanting to hire me but not having the courage quite yet. So I wouldn't give credence to that. Nobody came round.'

'Depending on the outcome of the post-mortem, we may have to come back and get a DNA sample from you,' Dunbar said, inwardly grimacing at the thought of anybody having to poke a swab into the man's mouth. They'd be lucky not to bring half a doughnut back out.

'No problem. I'll be here. I'm not going anywhere.'

Except in a box, sooner rather than later.

The detectives stood up. 'Thank you for your time, Mr Chalmers.'

'You know, we're all the same,' Chalmers said, picking up the doughnut again and taking a bite.

'What do you mean?' Dunbar asked.

'There's a hundred per cent chance that all three of us in this room are going to die one day. It just depends on how fast you want to go. Me? I'm lucky if I have five years, ten tops. The doc says I should think about picking out a box now. But I would rather enjoy myself on the way out than reach a grand old age where the only fun you have during the day is a good-looking nurse wiping your arse. I want to go to bed one night and not wake up.'

'Can't fault that logic,' Dunbar said, and he and Evans left the office.

'Cheery bastard, eh?' Evans said as they walked along the short hallway. The door to the outer office was ajar, and Agnes was still adjusting herself in her chair when Dunbar pushed the door.

'Cheers for now,' he said, about to walk past Agnes.

'I didn't tell him about the visit,' she said to the two policemen.

They stopped in their tracks. Agnes rolled her office chair to the door and closed it all the way.

'What visit?'

'The one I had here just shortly after Davie went missing. To be honest, I didn't know Chalmers that well, and I don't think I owe him anything. Sometimes he speaks to me like I'm a piece of gum on his shoe. So, he can get it right up himself.'

'Who visited you?' Dunbar pressed.

'A policeman. He wasn't in uniform, but he showed me his warrant card.'

'You get his name?'

'Chief Inspector Willie Munroe. He's based here, he said. He asked if I had heard from Davie. I told him, no, that Davie hadn't been here for a while. He asked me if it was unusual for him to be out of the office for so long. I told him it was. He asked if he could look at the files that Davie was last working on. I told him, not without a warrant. He left and I've never seen him again.'

'Willie Munroe. Thanks, Agnes.'

'Just don't tell his nibs that I told you. He doesn't know about it.'

'Our lips are sealed.'

They left the office.

SIXTEEN

The manse looked bigger than the church building, Harry thought as Chloe expertly guided the car through the stone pillars flanking the driveway.

There was a gravel drive in front of the church and the manse. They got out into the cool air and Harry looked around.

'I can update you later about my conversation with the inspector, but let's try and find this minister.'

'Okay.'

They walked up to the front door of the manse and rang the doorbell, but there was no answer.

'You hear that?' Harry asked Chloe.

'Looking for the minster?' a voice shouted. They

saw an old man standing behind the wrought-iron-topped wall, staring back at them.

'What gave it away?' Harry muttered to Chloe. 'The fact we're standing outside the minister's house?'

'Yes, we are,' Chloe shouted, smiling at the man.

'They have a rave every Monday,' he replied, pointing towards the back of the house.

'A what?' Harry said, walking closer.

'You know, a rave. Where the youngsters get together, get pished, and take drugs and dance until they choke on their own vomit. I haven't been to one, mind, but I'm not senile. I've seen it on TV.'

'And the minister holds a rave?' Harry said, looking round to see how close Chloe was, in case he had to ask her for help should the old man be on crack and decide to leap the fence.

'You can hear it now. Bang-bang-bang; the bloody music goes on all morning. Every Monday like clockwork. My wife would have pissed her pants if she knew what was going on. Long time deid, though, and I'm thankful she's at least spared it. That bloody racket would wake the dead.'

'Thanks for your help,' Harry said.

They walked across the little car park in front of what was clearly a church hall, the old man watching them as if they were going to set up a table outside and start selling drugs. Harry stood on the wide step and grabbed the door handle and the door opened towards them.

Inside, the music got louder, but it was hardly 'Firestarter' by the Prodigy. Although Harry didn't know if 'Firestarter' was played at any raves.

They walked round to their right and into the main church hall, where a bunch of men and women in various stages of unfitness were moving to the beat of the music. A woman stood at the front, teaching the class.

They all looked at the newcomers. A man at the back picked up a towel from a chair and walked over to them, wiping his face. He smiled as he approached.

'Good morning. I'm Reverend Baxter. James Baxter.'

'I'm Harry Mackay. My friend, Chloe Walker. Is there somewhere quieter we can chat? It's about Archie Spencer.'

'Let's walk round to the church.'

Baxter took out a key and opened the front door to the church, which led into a small vestibule before the main doors. 'It's a shame we have to keep it locked, but some people can't be led from temptation.'

Inside, it was cooler and their footsteps echoed.

'Take a pew. As it were,' Baxter said. He took the towel from his shoulder and wiped his face down again.

'Now, what is it I can help you with regarding Archie?' he asked as they sat down.

'We're trying to find out what happened to him,' Harry said.

Baxter's face took on a serious look. 'I can't even imagine what his mother went through. Nobody knows where he went. There's been lots of speculation, of course, but Archie's head was always in a science fiction book or a TV show. Nice lad, though. His mother asked me to keep him in mind if I heard of any jobs, so I gave him some work around here. He was the unofficial caretaker.'

'What about the other two people who went missing?' Chloe asked.

Baxter's eyebrows knitted together for a moment, as if he was annoyed that she had joined in the conversation. 'You're the artist, aren't you?' he said to her.

'Yes, I am.'

'Can I ask why you're so interested in Archie all of a sudden?'

'We know it's coming up to a year since they went missing. We were just interested, that's all,' Harry said, jumping in.

Baxter nodded, still looking closely at Chloe.

'What do you know about the Autumn Bonanza at the Corcoran estate?' Harry asked.

'I haven't heard of it, to be honest. This is a small town and we tend to stick to ourselves. My big day out is a trip up to Ayr some weekends with my wife. Do some shopping. Or if we're adventurous, we head up to Glasgow, but that's only now and again. I have to tend my flock.'

'I understand,' Harry said. 'Did you know the other two people who went missing?' He had noticed that Baxter had changed the subject.

'Nope. Didn't know any of them. Not even the private investigator who came snooping around here.'

'Jack Easton was a friend of Archie's. He came here to meet up with him. They were drinking in the bar of the Thistle, apparently.'

'They might have socialised in the Thistle, Mr Mackay, but they didn't attend the church here. We welcome visitors, but praising God wasn't on their agenda.'

They chatted for a few more minutes, then Harry stood up, and Chloe took her cue from him.

'Thank you for your time, Reverend Baxter.'

'Any time. And of course, my door is always open, especially on a Sunday.'

'I'll bear that in mind.'

Outside, it was starting to spit rain.

'I am capable of answering for myself, Harry,' Chloe said as they got back into the car.

'Don't say anything else just now. Just sit and smile.'

He gave Baxter a quick wave as Chloe turned the car around. The minister was standing in the doorway of the church and he smiled and waved back.

Harry saw him take his mobile phone out as he turned back into the church and then the door was closed.

'I didn't mean to jump in,' Harry said. 'Well, actually, I did. You saw the way he changed the subject. That's classic. He was trying psychology. Guiding the conversation round to his way. Manipulating us.'

'Oh, Harry, he's a minister.'

'Trust me, I've seen guys like him before.'

'Where to now?'

'Home. I want to check on the others.'

Just as Chloe was following the road round, Harry's phone rang, and for a minute, he thought it was the minister.

'Hello?'

'Harry, it's me, Jimmy. I'm calling with an update.'

'Liam McDonald's on the run and there's a bounty on his head?'

Chloe looked over to him. He shook his head at her.

'Nah, you're alright there. They all checked out. However, me and the boy were up at Loch Lomond today. We got a shout.'

'Oh, aye?'

'Aye. There was a body dug up out of a graveyard and dumped down by the shore. It was Davie Wylie.'

'Murdered?'

'Absolutely. I'm going to talk to Muckle, then we're going to the mortuary. I'd like to get together for a wee chinwag. Seems like we have to exchange notes, pal.'

'You coming down today?'

'Aye. But it will be later. Me and the boy might crash at your place, if you can spare us.'

'I have the McDonalds staying at my place. You could crash on the couch. It will be tight, but –'

'We'll wing it when we're down there. I know it's not that far from Glasgow, but by God, I could do with a pint. And when I've had a few, it's like being on a rollercoaster with Robbie driving.'

'You know I'm right here,' Robbie Evans said, his voice sounding far away.

'We'll sort something out. Let me know when you're on your way.'

'Will do, mucker.'

Harry hung up, thinking about how he might have to tell the others he was a police officer if Jimmy Dunbar did come down.

Oh well, he thought, *it was fun while it lasted.*

SEVENTEEN

'I can't find my night-time pills,' the old man said. The former Lord Corcoran looked at his son, who had inherited the title from his father.

'That's because it's only lunchtime, Dad.'

'Oh bugger. Give me a whisky instead, then.'

The old man's nurse, who followed him about all day like she was a dog, looked over at Corcoran and shook her head slightly. Corcoran was a man who rarely took orders from other people, but this woman was paid to look after the old man, and he didn't want his father running about in the garden again, wearing just his underpants and screaming and shouting. When it came to his father's well-being, the woman knew best.

'Nope. No whisky.'

'Did she tell you not to give me one?'

'If by *she* you mean Phyllis, then no. I'm telling you: behave yourself, or you'll have to go and watch television in the special room.'

The old man tutted and the nurse nodded to Corcoran and they left the room.

Corcoran shook his head and blew out a breath. 'It gets harder every day, I swear,' he said to the man who had been sitting quietly in one of the leather wingback chairs.

'I can imagine.' Colonel was sitting with an amused look on his face. 'He's a great guy. I like him a lot. I remember the fun we used to have.'

'Me too, but his mind is away now. No more fun and games for him.'

'Pity. He would have enjoyed this upcoming week. I remember when he used to foam at the mouth just thinking about it.'

Corcoran blew out a breath and stood up. 'Just because the old man's doolally, doesn't mean we can't have a whisky or two, does it?'

Colonel smiled. 'Indeed it does not.'

Both men were in their late fifties now, their livers either tolerant of the excessive drinking or well on their way to checking out.

Corcoran walked over to the large sideboard over

on one wall. The size of the room made it look small. He often thought that a television company could have come in here and filmed a TV series, if it hadn't been for the family secrets. It wouldn't do to have somebody snooping about the place. No, that wouldn't do at all.

He poured the whiskies from a decanter. He couldn't remember what the name of the stuff was, but at the end of the day, did it really matter? It would help them get blootered and then they would flush it away. The main thing was, it had to taste good when it went over the tongue, and this stuff did the job.

'I've gone over the guest list again,' Corcoran said, not for the first time. He had been going over the list again and again, ever since the RSVPs had come in.

'Bennington still not coming?' Colonel said, accepting the glass.

'No. Can you believe that? After all I've done for the bastard.' Corcoran sat down and shook his head, staring off into space for a moment. 'That's it, though; he's never coming here again.'

'I did hear his wife died just a couple of weeks ago.'

'Good. Serves the bastard right!' Corcoran said.

Colonel sprayed whisky out of his mouth and choked for a second before he burst out laughing. He wiped his mouth with the back of his hand. 'Jesus, Corky.'

'Fuck's sake. I wish you wouldn't do that,' Corcoran said, wiping some of the airborne whisky off his cheek. 'My fucking carpet was just cleaned.'

Colonel laughed again. 'Poor Bennington. Wife pops her clogs and old Corky is pissed off. The man can't catch a break.'

'I mean it, though. If I'm ever slighted, then God help the slighter.' Corcoran wasn't sure if that was an actual word or not, but it fitted Bennington to a T right now.

Corcoran was the only one who could chastise Colonel for unloading the contents of his mouth onto the Turkish rug. Even then, those little few hairs on the back of Corcoran's neck refused to lie down and die whenever he opened his mouth. They were up now, ready to do whatever it was hairs on the back of the neck did when called into action.

The smile fell off Colonel's face like a piece of loose rock off a cliff. One minute it was there, the next, gone.

'You want me to take care of him?'

Corcoran looked at the man in the opposite

chair, looking for any sign that at any minute a laugh would burst forth and he would be assured the other man was joking. But the laughter didn't come.

'No, no, it's fine. I'll just spread the word about how he's an antisocial bastard and the rest will take care of itself.'

'Is Sir Alan Diamond coming?' Colonel asked, his smile wrapping itself around the crystal tumbler again.

'Yes, he is! Diamond Geezer was one of the first to reply. I can always count on him. When people see he's coming, they try to make sure they attend. Big deals are going to be made this year, Colonel. Stocks in my businesses are going to skyrocket. Prices of everything are going up, which means our profit margins are going to increase too. This is going to be the best bonanza we've ever had.'

'You don't think Bennington will talk, do you?' Colonel asked.

'He's a prominent Scottish businessman. He knows which side his bread is buttered on.' As Corcoran spoke the words, there was no conviction there.

'I hope so. You know what happened last year.'

'An unfortunate incident. But it was taken care

of.' Corcoran knew what the other man was going to say before the words came out of his mouth.

'What about the other problem we have?'

Corcoran drank some more whisky and tapped his fingers on the arm of the leather chair, a drumbeat to a tune only he knew. 'I still want to go ahead with it. It was the plan. The time is right. Besides, if those interfering people had kept their noses out, they wouldn't have been taken care of the way they were.'

'It's true. It's going to be a great centrepiece this year.' This time, Colonel took a drink without blowing it everywhere. 'I have to admire the way you have these people in your hand, Corky.'

'At the end of the day, we all gain something, and that's what counts.'

Corcoran's phone rang. He took it out of his pocket and answered it. 'Speak.'

'It's me. I just heard through the grapevine that Davie Wylie's been found.'

Corcoran was quiet for a moment before answering. 'Where and when?'

'Loch Lomond, earlier today. I don't know all the details, but it looks like he was buried somewhere and dug up. Then left on the shore in full view of the tourists.'

'Jesus. We need to talk about this in private. Don't call this number again. Call Colonel in future.'

'Yes, sir,' the man replied, then he hung up.

'You're never going to guess,' Corcoran said.

'Give me a clue.'

'Davie Wylie was dug up from somewhere and left on the shore of Loch Lomond.'

'You said guess. You didn't even give me a chance.'

'Is that what you were going to say? "Oh, I think Davie Wylie was dug up and dumped at Loch Lomond"?'

'Might have been.'

'Well, you would have been right. But that creates a problem.'

Colonel shrugged. 'Let's not jump the gun. There might be a perfectly acceptable reason.'

'Can you contact your friend and ask him?'

'He's hardly a friend, and no. He's not the sort of man you question. It's not like, "I told you to wash my car and you missed a spot." He wouldn't take kindly to that.'

'Maybe you could use somebody less touchy next time then.'

'I'll tell him that when he calls looking for work, shall I?'

'Don't be a smartarse.' The hairs were still up on Corcoran's neck, but he had to keep control.

'I'll call what's-his-name. He'd better bloody well have some kind of answer.'

Corcoran knew Colonel was passing the buck, but so what? As long as things got sorted.

EIGHTEEN

Chloe was still pissed off at him, he could tell. She put her foot down when they were going up their road.

'You're still angry, I can tell,' he said.

'I'm not, Harry, but I'm a big girl.'

'I know that. It was just instinct.' *And the fact that I'm a copper so they were going to listen to me.*

'It's fine. I'll get over it. I just got the feeling they were humouring me in there. Muddy boots in the kitchen? Should we call in the murder squad?'

She pulled into Harry's drive behind the van. Harry was driving the Ford Mondeo that belonged to Jessica. He had swapped Alex's car for it, just to drive around in. If anybody ran the plates, his name wouldn't come up.

Inside the house, it was a complete one-eighty from what it was usually like. There was noise from the TV, Alice was squealing as Lisa played with her and something was going on in the kitchen.

'Just in time for lunch,' Liam said, coming through to the living room. 'I'm making soup. Homemade lentil. It tastes good but will make you fart like thunder.'

'Sounds good to me,' Harry said. 'The soup thing, not the farting.'

'Hi,' Lisa said when she caught hold of Alice.

'Hi, Harry!' Alice said, giving him her toy cat. 'You want to play dolls with me?'

'Of course I do. Wait till I take off my jacket, then we'll get the dolls out.'

'Yay!' She ran away to the stairs, her feet clomping on the wood.

'You don't have to,' Lisa said.

'Of course he does,' Chloe said. 'He's committed now.'

'I do. It's not a problem.' He hung his jacket up and Alice came back with some dolls, and he sat on the floor with her, having fun.

He thought of his own little girl and felt a stab of something inside. Guilt? Worry? Love? All the above, he decided.

Chloe chatted with Lisa in front of the TV while Liam clanged about in the kitchen.

When the soup was ready, Liam brought the bowls out and served it up, while Harry promised Alice there was room at the table for the dolls.

'This is good, Liam,' Harry said, meaning it. The soup was thick and tasted delicious. 'I didn't think I had lentils in the house.'

'You didn't. I nipped along to Sainsbury's and bought what we needed.'

'Let me square you up for the cost.'

'There's no need.'

'Yes, there is. I insist. I'll give you the money when we're done.'

'Thanks, fella, but there really was no need.'

Harry waved him away and got tucked into the soup.

'How did you get on this morning?' Lisa asked.

'Nothing much from the inspector in town,' Harry said. 'He did tell me that Archie Spencer worked in the church, part-time. We spoke to the minister, but he wasn't too informative.'

'We saw him in the fitness class,' Chloe said.

'Oh yes, people around here love him,' Lisa said.

'Archie worked there,' Harry said, 'but Baxter didn't seem interested that he disappeared.'

'Doesn't surprise me, son,' Liam said. 'I wouldn't trust him as far as I could spit him.'

'What do you know about the Autumn Bonanza?'

'It's some fair thing they have at the Corcoran estate round at Barlae,' Lisa said. 'It's a big to-do, with politicians and celebrities attending. Businessmen and the like. Very tight security.'

'It's locked down tighter than a crab's arse,' Liam said.

'Grandad,' Lisa said, nodding to Alice.

'Sorry, hen.' Liam ducked his head down and scooped more soup into his mouth.

'How do we find out who's invited?' Harry asked.

'You don't. It's not public.'

'I'm going to have a word with Archie Spencer's mother this afternoon,' Harry said.

'That should be interesting,' Lisa said. 'She told us nothing.'

NINETEEN

Corcoran Senior walked ahead of the nurse, a middle-aged woman called Phyllis, down the stairs that led into the basement. Or *wine cellar* as his pompous son called it. Senior wasn't a wine drinker at all. Wouldn't use it to clean the toilet with.

'Please be careful, Senior,' Phyllis said. Or Phil, as Senior insisted on calling her.

'I'm fine, Phil. Just keep an eye out for one of those nosey sods who'll go running back to my son. They forget that I was once king of the castle. I still have clout with that little bastard upstairs. They shouldn't forget that. I know you won't, eh?' He chuckled.

Phyllis had been entertaining one of the delivery men one afternoon when she was supposed to be keeping an eye on Senior. She'd thought the old man was napping, but he wasn't, he was wandering. He'd managed to go for a piss all by himself, despite his son's scepticism that his father could put out his shoelaces if they were on fire. It didn't do any harm to let him think he was dafter than he really was.

They reached the bottom of the stairs, where dim lights shone from the walls. A switch would put more on, but this was in case some dafty came down half-jaked and forgot to put a light on and fell. Not that his son would worry if some bastard broke his neck. He was more concerned about losing a valuable bottle of wine.

Along to the end and turning left, they walked past thousands of pounds' worth of alcohol. Rack upon rack. Senior didn't know where his son got his penchant for wine. It certainly wasn't from him. Probably some of those jumped-up ponces who came to the Bonanza. Another little idea his son had.

They came to an end rack and Senior stopped before it and pulled on it. These bottles were empty and glued onto the rack. Just for show, they kept prying eyes from what was behind this rack. It had once been a door but had been changed by His Lordship upstairs. Senior pushed against it and something clicked and it swung inwards.

This corridor was colder because there were no windows in here. His son had told him that once upon a time, prisoners would be brought down here and tortured and flogged. Somewhere along the line, some jail cells had been built.

There was an archway at the end that opened up into a large subterranean room. For exercise.

Phyllis followed with the chessboard and pieces. One of the empty cells had a table in it and a couple of folding chairs. Senior dragged them out and set the table up in the exercise room.

Then Phyllis unlocked the door to another cell and opened it. There was an open rectangle in it and a big enough gap at the bottom to slide a food tray under, but this prisoner didn't give anybody any hassle.

The door swung in and the boy got to his feet. He gave Senior a slight smile, the only clue that he was pleased to see him.

'Come on, son. Let's go and play our game.'

'Coming,' Henry McDonald said, stretching his arms above his head and yawning.

'Did you enjoy your birthday cake?' Phyllis asked.

'Yes. Thank you.'

'It wasn't much, but we thought you would like it. It's not every day you turn eighteen, is it?'

'No.'

Henry was a boy – now a man – of few words. He shuffled out and helped Senior set up the chessboard on the table.

'Let's play,' Senior said when Henry sat down.

TWENTY

Muckle McInsh was a former detective inspector who'd worked under Jimmy Dunbar back in the day. After working various security jobs, he had teamed up with a couple of friends and created the Night Watch Security business. It was in a former shop not far from Helen Street station.

'Watch that caravan!' Dunbar shouted out, pointing to a small food trailer across the road.

'You're not even funny,' Evans said, turning the engine off.

Dunbar chuckled. 'Go and get us a couple of burgers, son,' he said, handing over some money.

'Usual?'

'Aye. Ketchup. And tell that wee bastard Tony he'd better have washed his hands.'

'They wear nitrile gloves now.'

'People can't scratch their arse with gloves on?'

The name of the business was painted on the shop window. The bottom half of the window had been made opaque with a couple of coats of paint, and net curtains gave privacy at the top. Dunbar knocked and the secretary got up from behind her desk and unlocked it.

'Hey, Maggie. How's life treating you?'

'Oh, you know. Still single. Still broke with the wages Muckle pays me. How's my favourite DCI?'

'Hungry, just as broke as you are, but alas, I'm still married.'

Maggie shut the door behind him.

'Robbie's getting us scran,' he said, so she kept it unlocked.

'A woman can only dream, Jimmy. It's been a long time since I met an eligible man who still had his own teeth and didn't have to comb his hair over the top of his baldy heid.'

'There's not many of us left.' He heard Sparky starting to bark behind a closed door.

'The Hardy Boys are through there waiting for you. And Nancy Drew too.'

'We can hear you,' Muckle shouted through and that set the German Shepherd off good and proper.

'I don't keep it a secret what I call you behind your back.'

'She's got a point,' Shug said.

Dunbar opened the door and shouted, 'Sparks, my boy.' The dog stopped his killer attack mode just in time to get his ears rubbed by Dunbar, his tail giving it yahoo.

'Hi, Jimmy,' Vern said, smiling at him.

'Hi, Vern.'

'Dr Watson will be right behind Sherlock,' Maggie said.

'Aw, come on, Mags. I didn't think you had a name for us too,' Dunbar complained.

'Sherlock's through there with the rest of the A-Team,' she said to Evans as he came in.

'Thanks, Maggie.'

'You're still single, aren't you, Robbie?' Maggie said.

'No, he isn't,' Vern shouted.

Evans felt his face going red. 'Be a love and close the door, will you?' he said to her.

'What do you think I am? A secretary?' She grinned at him.

'Yes!' Muckle shouted.

Evans held the food aloft as the dog eyed it up.

'Sparky, go lie down,' Muckle ordered, and the

dog ran into the corner where his bed was, but he kept his eyes on the food.

There were three desks in the big room, all with computer screens. There were a couple of spare chairs and the detectives sat down. Vern and Evans began chatting.

'How was your trip to Loch Lomond?' Shug asked. He was a small man and had his office chair cranked up high.

'It would have been nice if it wasn't for the remains of Davie Wylie lying with his head blown off.'

Evans turned to look at Dunbar, his hamburger roll halfway to his mouth.

'What?' Dunbar said, taking a bite out of his own roll. 'You were there. You saw him.'

'I was going to get a salad, but oh no, I thought, I'll have a hamburger for a change,' Evans said. 'Suddenly, I've lost my appetite.'

'His brains looked a bit like this meat,' Dunbar said.

'Oh Christ, now I'm no' hungry at all.'

'I'll take it,' Vern said, grinning. Evans passed his lunch over.

'You wanted to talk to me about Wylie?' Muckle

asked. Real name Michael McInsh, he was a big man, hence the nickname.

'Aye. Since he was one of us at one time, just like you. And then he was in your game.'

'To be honest, I only spoke to him a few times. He was a good guy, though. Hated it when the big companies tried to screw the little man. He didn't take any guff off anybody.'

'Like you,' Dunbar said between mouthfuls.

'Exactly.'

'Did he ever talk to you about going down to Newton Stewart?'

'No. The last I heard he had gone down there and disappeared. From what I could learn, it wasn't like he had run off with a great deal of money, so we figured it had something to do with the case.'

'His business partner seems to think he did. But I think you're right. From what we can gather, Wylie was a pretty straight-up bloke. What about Willie Munroe?' Dunbar took another bite out of his roll.

'Munroe?' Muckle spluttered. 'Jesus, that's a name I haven't heard in a long time. I thought he would have been retired by now.'

'No such luck, Muckle, son. Bad bastard that he is. I've never met anybody who said they liked him.'

'Me neither.'

Dunbar said to Shug, 'Your husband's good at the computers. You should look him up. Maybe under the radar. You'll see what a piece of slime he is.'

'Does he have any connection to Wylie?' Shug asked.

'Wylie used to be a DI in the same station as Munroe. Everybody hated Munroe. He has a big mouth; that's why he only made it as far as chief inspector. He could have gone far, but he has a poor record,' Dunbar said.

'He was in charge of the missing persons' case.'

'Why was Glasgow involved?' Shug asked.

'The report was made here, and the missing people were from here. Anyway, he took charge and nothing was done.'

'He sounds like a real piece of work,' Shug said.

'He is. He's younger than me, so he should be retiring soon because he's in uniform. Good riddance to him.'

'I'd raise a glass to that,' Muckle said and Sparky perked his ears up. 'Settle down, boy. Stop earwigging. Or I'll change your name to Maggie.'

'I heard that!' Maggie shouted through.

'That just proved my point!'

Dunbar stood up. 'Me and the boy have to go to

the mortuary, but can I have a wee word outside? No offence to either of you,' he said, nodding to Vern and Shug.

'Go right ahead, boss; I've got work to do,' Shug said, getting back to his keyboard. Vern just smiled and went back to talking to Evans. Sparky sat and waited for the command to come, but Muckle told him to stay instead. The dog's ears perked up and Dunbar thought the German Shepherd might entertain himself by ripping his doggy bed to shreds while he waited.

Outside, it was cold and windy. 'Listen, son, sometimes things are on a need-to-know basis,' said Dunbar. 'Well, there's something I need you to know.'

TWENTY-ONE

The guest house was just along from the church where Harry and Chloe had been earlier. It was tucked away from the road up a little gravel driveway.

'There are vacancies here,' Harry said. 'Might be a nice place to stay for somebody coming down here for a visit.'

'I used to prefer the lights and sounds of Glasgow until –' She suddenly stopped talking and stared ahead out of the windscreen as she guided the little car up into the car park.

'Until?' Harry prompted.

'What? Oh, nothing. Just thinking about my ex.' She turned to look at him. 'I wanted a breath of fresh air, which I got down here. It was either that or up in the Highlands. You ever been there?'

'I was born there. Inverness. We moved when I was twelve.'

'You'll be biased towards it then.'

'It holds no special memories, to be honest.'

The gravel crunched under the tyres as she pulled to a stop near the front door. The sign hanging outside on the wall read, *Hilltop Guest House.* It was a red-stone, solid-looking house that had probably been there well before the houses nearby.

They crunched their way across to the front door, which was open. There was another glass door facing them and they went in. A little bell dinged above their heads, like a boxing match was going to break out. The smell was clean, like a can of furniture polish had exploded.

'Good afternoon. How can I help you?' a woman said, coming out of a room.

Harry introduced them, then said, 'We're looking for Mrs Spencer.'

'And you are?' The smile slipped a little bit.

'We're friends of Jack Easton. He went missing here a year ago.'

'Oh yes, yes, I remember that. But what has that got to do with me?'

'Your son was a friend of his, was he not?' Chloe asked.

'Oh yes, of course. Sorry. Silly me. Please, come through to the back of the house and we can have some tea.'

She turned on her heel and marched towards another doorway and led them through into her own quarters. They sat down on a couch in her living room.

'What do you take in your tea?' Mrs Spencer said.

'It's fine,' Harry said. 'We really don't have time. We were hoping you could help us find our friend. Nobody is bothering to look anymore.'

'You're the artist who lives along the road, aren't you?' Mrs Spencer said to Chloe.

In a small town, along the road was just that. A hop, skip and a jump and you were at the opposite end of the town. Like it was a sort of time travel without the aid of a police box.

Chloe nodded. 'Yes. I live near Harry.'

'I've seen you around. People seem to like your work.' Mrs Spencer's tone suggested that she herself thought Chloe's paintings were a load of pish, and this view seemed to be confirmed when Harry saw none of Chloe's paintings hanging on the walls. There was a seascape that could have been a painting-by-numbers, and another one of Big Ben in London, and when Harry stared at it a bit longer, he could see it was a jigsaw puzzle glued together and shoved behind a frame. Very classy.

'I told the police everything I know a year ago. I don't see what this rehashing everything will get except dredging up bad memories. Archie's gone and he isn't coming back.'

Harry had confirmed with Jimmy Dunbar that nothing of Spencer's had been used since he disappeared – no bank cards, nothing. It was like he'd completely disappeared off the face of the earth.

Which might buy into his spaceman conspiracy theories. Maybe he'd had a microscope shoved up his arse on the mothership or been made to impregnate some alien women. But from what he had heard of Archie, the young man probably would have enjoyed doing that.

'How did he know Jack?' Harry said, not letting go just yet.

'Jack was a journalist. He worked on investigations. You know, snooping about on other people's property, exposing corrupt builders, that sort of thing. Archie found him online, apparently, and they struck up a friendship.'

'Jack brought his brother-in-law the weekend they went missing. He was meeting Archie. Did Archie talk about it before they went to the wildlife centre?' Harry asked.

'Archie's a grown man. He doesn't have to tell me anything. I showed him respect when he was growing up, taught him boundaries.'

'How did he become interested in conspiracy theories?' Chloe asked.

Something shifted on Mrs Spencer's face, as if a light bulb had just gone on in her head. 'I don't have to answer your questions. You're not even police officers. I want you to go.'

She suddenly stood up. 'Get out of my house and never come back here again. If you do, I'll call the police.'

Harry looked at Chloe, then at Mrs Spencer. 'Please understand we're just trying to find our friend.' He stood up and Chloe followed suit.

'There's nothing I can do about getting your friend back.'

'No, Mum, but there's something I can do,' Archie Spencer said from the doorway.

TWENTY-TWO

'The mortuary is invariably in the basement of a hospital,' Evans said as they took the lift down in the Queen Elizabeth University Hospital building in Glasgow.

'The one in Edinburgh isn't,' Dunbar said.

'Most of them are, though. Even hospitals in Edinburgh have mortuaries.'

'This one works with us and the PF. And stop trying to sound like you know what you're talking about.'

'What's twisting your Y-fronts? You've been moody ever since we left Muckle's office,' Evans said.

'Aye, I know. Just the sound of that bastard's name gets me revved up. Willie Munroe. He's always trouble.'

'Don't let it ruin your day, boss.'

'Too late for that, son. But let's go and see how Davie Wylie's cleaned up.'

They got out of the lift and turned left, heading along to the mortuary. Then Dunbar saw a familiar face as he opened the stairwell door and disappeared through it. Willie Munroe.

He rushed along to the door and opened it, only to hear a door somewhere else closing.

'He moves fast for a fat bastard,' Dunbar said, not wanting to run up the stairs after the man. Stairs were meant for going down; the lift was meant for going up. 'Come on, Robbie, let's see what that arsehole was up to.'

It was a big place with a lot of staff. They had labs and the like, but the place Dunbar was looking for was where the cadavers were cut up.

He found Fiona Christie in the postmortem suite.

'The inimitable Jimmy Dunbar. We meet again. Don't worry, you'll get invited to the Christmas party.'

'More dancing on the tables?' Robbie said. 'We wouldn't want him falling and breaking a hip.'

'Shut up,' Dunbar said. Then to Fiona: 'I saw

Chief Inspector Willie Munroe leaving here a minute ago.'

'Yes, he was here. You know, if he was the first policeman I met, I wouldn't be impressed. He doesn't give the force a very good reputation.'

'Was he being lippy?'

'Obnoxious, yes. Demanding to know the results of the post-mortem. I had a shock for him: Mr Wylie is scheduled for tomorrow now. I had two sudden deaths come in. But one thing I will say: I did an initial examination of him, and I'm shocked. And believe me, I'm old enough now to not be shocked at a crime scene.'

The two detectives waited out the pause for dramatic effect. When Fiona judged a suitable amount of time had passed, she carried on.

'I think the shotgun blast killed him, but there are several other injuries to him that would have hurt like hell. Not fatal, but very painful.'

'What's that?'

'He'd been shot with a bow and arrow. Maybe a crossbow. Several times. There was an arrowhead stuck in his right femur. Broken off from the shaft.'

'How many, Doc?' Dunbar asked. It took a lot to shock him, but this sent a shiver down his back.

'Four. One in his arm, three in his legs. Only one

broken, though. Not enough to kill him, but certainly enough to cause a lot of pain.'

'He was tortured?' Evans said.

'That's what I would conclude.'

Dunbar shook his head. 'He was shot with a crossbow, and then somebody took him out with a shotgun?'

'That's what I'm guessing. Also, on his head? There are little pieces of plastic. I wondered what they were at first. Most of them are black. Then I had a closer look. There was the tiniest piece of motherboard in there.'

'Motherboard?' Evans asked.

'Like he was using a phone when the shotgun blast took him out,' Dunbar said.

'There wasn't a phone on him, so maybe the killer shot him and then took the remains of it.'

'Thanks, Fiona. If you could call Tom Barclay when Wylie is ready to have his day on the table, I'd appreciate it. He'll be along with Sylvia McGuire.'

'No problem.'

'Can I ask you: did you tell Willie Munroe any of this?'

Fiona shook her head. 'No. I just told him it hadn't started yet. He wanted to send a couple of his officers, but I told him that you had already dealt with that. He seemed furious. To be honest, he's a bit scary when he goes like that. He was muttering away to himself when he left. I heard him say, "Not if I have anything to do with it."'

'Did he now? I might have to have a wee chat with him.'

'There's something else I didn't tell him, something that you will find interesting, I'm sure.'

'I'm all ears.'

'The woman they found in the coffin in the grave where Wylie was dug up?'

'What about her?' Dunbar asked.

'It's not her grave. The headstone said the occupant was Victoria Treadwell, who died in nineteen ninety, aged seventy-two. This woman was younger, wearing jeans and had a money clip in her pocket, along with her driving licence. Sarah Marshall, aged twenty-one. Address in Newton Stewart. I've done some scrapings from under her fingernails and my lab is going to run the DNA.'

'Thanks, Fiona. If you need me for anything, just call.'

'Vodka and Coke in your usual bar?'

'Next time I'm going, I'll give you a shout.'

Dunbar and Evans left the autopsy suite.

'Jesus, the pathologist flirting with you? The formaldehyde must be going to her heid.'

'We're just colleagues, ya wee baw bag.'

Outside, Dunbar was watchful, keeping an eye out for Munroe, but the other man didn't show his face.

'Just keep your wits about you, son,' he said. 'There have been rumours about Munroe for years. He's a bad bastard.'

'He doesn't worry me, boss.'

'Me neither, but he doesn't fight fair. He has a crew with him. Some other uniforms. I've heard stories, but nothing that would hold up in court. And to be honest, Robbie, that fucking bow-and-arrow story puts me on edge.'

'Do you still carry your wee blackjack?'

'Aye. Fucking always. You?'

'You taught me well, boss.'

'Good lad. Now, did you have any plans with Vern tonight?'

'Aye, I did.'

'Well, when she calls you, act surprised. Your date's been cancelled.'

'Oh, what?' Evans made a face.

'My decision, not hers.'

'Cheers for that. As much as I like your

company, I'm not going dancing with you. Keep that nonsense for Dr Fiona.'

'Aye, keep sayin' that so my Cathy hears about it and thinks there's something going on. Then I'll get booted out.'

'You shouldn't be thinking about diddling the doctor, then.'

'Shut your hole. If I do get booted out, I'll ask my friend Vern if I can crash at her place. Then see how much privacy you'll have.'

'You wouldn't.' Evans made a face like his worst nightmare had just come true.

'I'd even let you spoon with Scooby.'

'Where did you say we were going, boss?'

'We're going to visit a friend of ours. Not far away, but you might want to pack some skids. I have a feeling this is not going to be over quickly.'

TWENTY-THREE

They sat in the gazebo, surrounding by bushes and high walls. Archie Spencer had told his mother that she should stay inside. This was just between himself, Harry and Chloe.

It was sheltered in here, but Chloe was still shaking.

'A lot of people were looking for you, son,' Harry said, trying to keep the irritation out of his voice.

'I know. But some of them are the wrong people.' Archie was in his mid-twenties with long hair and glasses. He looked like the stereotypical nerd from TV.

'Who?' Harry asked.

Archie looked at him, and Harry could see grey

hairs in among the light brown. There were lines round his eyes.

'The people who killed Jack Easton and his brother-in-law.'

Harry heard Chloe take a breath in and hold it there. He looked over at her and saw tears forming in her eyes. 'How do you know Jack and Henry are dead?' she asked, her voice a scratchy whisper.

'I heard them being shot dead.'

'Tell us about that day,' Harry said, his heart beating faster. He knew Lisa was going to be devastated, but he wasn't going to mention it just yet. 'Start off with how you got involved with Jack Easton.'

Archie sat with his arms on his legs, hands clasped together, looking down at the grass. Harry saw his mother looking out of a window. She ducked back inside when she saw him looking.

Then Archie sat up again. 'Jack and I met on a website for disbelievers. You know, people who don't believe the government shite. "There are no aliens." "An iceberg sank the *Titanic*." That sort of stuff. There are departments within the government that specialise just in misinformation. We got talking and he was a great guy. He was a disbeliever like me. He'd started to hate the establishment, just like I do.

One of the biggest proponents of the lie factory is Lord Corcoran. He has an estate to the north of here. It's his family home, but he lives in London most of the time. He holds an annual Autumn Bonanza. It's where his like-minded cronies turn up for God-knows-what. He's been heard saying he based his idea on Bohemian Grove in California.'

'A gathering of famous people,' Harry said.

'Yes. You heard of it?'

Harry didn't want to tell him he only knew of it because of Inspector Robertson. 'Yes,' he said.

'There are some mad rumours going about online about what goes on in the Corcoran estate, by people who claim to have sneaked in and witnessed all sorts of bollocks. Including human sacrifice.'

Harry looked at Chloe, who seemed to be in a daze. Maybe this questioning thing wasn't for her. 'Do you want to go home?' he asked her.

She shook her head. But couldn't speak for a moment. 'No, I'll be fine.'

Harry looked back at Archie. 'Carry on, son.'

'Aye. So one of the things that somebody claimed to have seen was a raft being set on fire and pushed out into the small loch that's on the property. Dark Loch, it's called. This raft had somebody on it. Alive. They were burnt on the raft and either died or were left to drown. Then a boat went out the next morning and cleared everything up. I wanted to see for myself just what goes on there. So did Jack.'

'Let me guess: he came down here to meet you and you showed him around the Galloway Wildlife Centre.'

'I did. We went during the day first, so we could get a feel for the layout of the place. So we could get a good view of Corcoran's estate. We came back here, had a few beers and arranged to go back the following day, late. Just before sunset. Then we would go up in the dark. You see, the centre lets you look at the stars without them being washed out by city lights. It's the perfect place to spot UFOs. But there's a spot where you can look right down into the estate. You can't see the big house for all the trees, only one of the other houses that are dotted around on the land. I knew that because I'd been the week before. One window. That's what I saw. One window, and a woman being murdered in that room.'

Harry looked at him for a moment to see if he was being serious. He was.

'Can you be sure?' he asked.

Now Archie had tears in his eyes and he took off his glasses to wipe his eyes. 'I know she got in there. She was a friend of mine. Sarah Marshall. She wanted to get in and she managed it. But I saw her being murdered by somebody. He took her by surprise and she didn't have a chance. I called the police and told them. They sent a car to the house and one up to the centre. I was waiting for them there. Then a black SUV came up. Four men got out, casual, like. They were watching us and I knew, just knew, it was those bastards from the house. Some of the security men. But the policemen didn't do anything. Her car was with me. They left and told me I could be charged with wasting police time. The men in the black car also left.'

'When did this happen exactly?'

'A week before Jack came down. I was in full meltdown mode.'

'Does Sarah have family?' Harry asked.

Archie shook his head. 'She rented a wee place along the road. Her parents are dead and she has no other family.'

'There must be normal people getting in there. Like delivery drivers,' Harry said.

'There are two small forests, one surrounding the main house, and the other where they have the guest cabins. There's also a building there that accepts all the deliveries, and then whatever's needed up at the main house is transported up there by staff.'

'What happened the night Jack and Henry disappeared?' Chloe asked.

'We went to the centre. There were a number of cars there. It was after dark and a lot of astronomers and photographers go there after dark. Some of them hoping to spot something not from this planet. It's well-documented that people have spotted UFOs there.'

'Why in God's name did you take Henry with you?' Chloe said, anger in her voice.

'It was Jack's idea. He said we would blend in more if we had the boy with us. Just some friends up to gaze at the stars. I told him not to bring Henry, but he said it was the perfect cover.'

'That was the night they were murdered?' Harry asked.

'Yes. It was full dark and people had torches but were encouraged to keep them switched off so our eyes would adjust to the dark. I told Jack where to look with his telescope he had brought. We were out in the car park when the black SUV came again.'

There was a haunted look in his eyes, as if he was replaying that night in his mind over and over.

'Take your time, Archie,' Harry said, putting his hand on the younger man's shoulder for a second.

Archie blew out a breath and composed himself again.

'They got out of their vehicle and were just wandering around, but I knew they were watching us. Then another car came up. Black again, with blacked-out windows. I turned and I said to Jack...'

TWENTY-FOUR

'...I don't like the look of those guys.' Archie Spencer tried not to look in their direction.

'Let's get inside,' Jack said. He put a hand on Henry's shoulder and gently guided him, but the men had their torches out and saw what he was doing.

'Get in the car,' Archie said, pointing to the old Land Rover 90 they had come in.

'Henry, this way,' Jack said, guiding the boy once more. The men in black anticipated their movement and headed to cut them off.

'Run!' Jack shouted suddenly and they sprinted for the car. One of the men in black got there first.

'Going somewhere?' he said.

'Aye, so get out of my fucking way,' Jack said.

The man smiled and turned to look at his colleagues. Jack knew this was the lead-up to the man punching him, so he stepped in close and head-butted him hard, breaking his nose. The man let out a yell and fell backwards.

Archie ducked behind the cars as the others ran across to help their friend. Henry took off down the hill, blending in with the darkness. Jack had made sure they all wore black.

Jack stuck it on one of the other men and dodged round the others as he took off after Henry.

Two men got out of the other car, looking at their colleagues.

'Don't just stand there – get fucking after them!' the older one barked. The man he was with started running too.

The darkness soon swallowed them up. Archie stayed hidden behind a car, then decided to walk with bent legs towards his own car.

Then he heard the unmistakable bangs as two shotgun blasts cut through the air.

Fear sent a jolt through him, and he stood up and ran towards his car. There was a light on outside the door of the centre, giving a muted glow to the car park. He was dismayed to see the second black car had pulled in right next to his Land Rover. There was nobody in it, the first man having taken off. The second was...where?

He took his car keys out and was trying to put the key in the lock when he heard a voice next to him.

'Hello, Archie.'

Colonel stood looking at the younger man. Archie looked at him, then put the key in the lock.

'You're not going anywhere, son.'

Archie's heart was going to explode. 'Is that right?'

'Sarah told us all about you. How you like to go snooping. I mean, she did so under duress. We did have her tied to a chair at the time. I think I had broken three of her fingers when she gave up. How many fingers will we have to break for you to spill the beans, I wonder?'

Archie wasn't a fighting man, but he stepped forward then, keeping his arm close to his body, and brought his fist up fast, connecting with Colonel's chin. The older man went down, making a gurgling sound.

Archie then took out a pocket knife and stabbed the front and back tyres on the passenger side of the black vehicle, before jumping into his car.

He put it into reverse and looked in the mirror and took a sharp intake of breath.

Colonel was standing right behind the big car, rubbing his jaw.

Archie could floor it and go right over the big man, but when push came to shove, he couldn't do it. What he *could* do was put the big car into four-wheel drive and take off. Which he did.

The car bumped down over the hill and Archie said a little prayer. Some of the men in black were running up the hill towards him, but he didn't stop. Several jumped up out of the way. He knew it wouldn't be long before they got into their own car and chased him.

He cut diagonally across the rough ground, the big vehicle jumping and bouncing, branches scratching at the car and the windows, but he focused on getting through the dark without any lights on.

Then he hit the road and shot right over to a grassy area and onto a pathway that cut through the trees. He had been up this path many times and knew where it would bring him out.

Suddenly, he was about to hit the one-lane road, so he jammed his brakes on, skidding to an almost halt. Then he turned onto the road, still keeping it dark. He crossed over the river and looked back through the window. He saw the lights from the pursuing car cutting through the trees and then it came down the road.

He carried straight on, the road bending round to the right, then left. Opposite a footpath was a solitary driveway leading to a house, on its own with no neighbours for miles. Great if you wanted to host a loud party, but if you dropped down of a heart attack, you were pretty much fucked.

He shot up the footpath, knowing there was an intersection ahead that went four ways. If he could get out of sight now, they wouldn't know which way he had gone.

He booted it up the footpath, the big machine bumping and swaying, but it was relentless at getting up the hill. He made it to the road and saw the headlights below cutting through the darkness. Then they stopped at the intersection.

While the old car could go anywhere, one attribute it lacked was quietness.

In his panic to get away, Archie gunned it. The noise of his old exhaust reverberated round Saturn's moons, it was so loud. He cursed himself for putting the foot down so soon as he saw the headlights from the other car turn in his direction.

He floored it, and to give the old girl her due, she picked up her skirts and booted it out of there. Archie knew he couldn't outrun that other, newer vehicle for long. He gave it the gun anyway, trying desperately to put some distance between him and his pursuers.

The old car could still shift and Archie dispensed with tickling the accelerator, instead giving it good old fucking stomping. Beyond that was the Bothy café. He needed to get there and then maybe he would have a chance.

The loch was dark and foreboding on his right, a huge entity that would swallow him up.

He booted over to the Bothy café and stopped his car. He took his backpack, turned off the engine – leaving the keys in the ignition – and ran and hid.

It was pitch black here. He kept quiet as the speeding car shot across the dam. The vehicle stopped at his Land Rover and now he could see one of the men had a rifle and two others had shotguns. The driver jumped out and started giving orders.

'Spread out! Find him.'

Archie took a ton of photos of the men as they were illuminated by their car's headlights.

After half an hour, they stopped searching. 'He must know this place like the back of his hand.

Never mind, we'll send somebody round to his address.'

Three men got into their car while one of them got into the Land Rover.

'Wait!' the driver instructed. There was a conflab and then they got into their car and drove off, leaving the Land Rover behind.

Archie waited for a long time, but he knew he'd need to leave before sunrise to keep under the cover of darkness.

When he was sure they were gone for good, he climbed out from underneath the black bags in the industrial bin outside the café. He thought about using the Land Rover to get home but knew they might be waiting down the road for him.

He would have to disappear, and leaving the Land Rover behind would help. He'd hiked these hills all his life and knew his way around them like a sailor knew his way around a French hoor's bedroom. If he could make it to the main road, he could find a farm and ask to use the telephone. Who he would call, he didn't quite know in that moment. All he knew was he had to get out of here.

He started the climb.

TWENTY-FIVE

'And you came back here, I assume,' Harry said to Archie.

'I did. I live up in the attic. The entrance to it is in a walk-in pantry. My dad built shelves onto the door when I was young. You wouldn't know it's there unless you looked really hard.'

'Did those guys come looking for you here?' Harry looked at Chloe, who seemed to be staring into space. He reached over and gave her hand a squeeze. She wrapped her fingers round his.

'They did. One of them pretended to be a friend of mine. My mother had reported me missing and told him so. Said she hadn't seen me since the night I had gone to the centre. The man left, but she saw a strange car parked in the street a few times over a couple of weeks. Then nothing.'

'The police had your car towed?'

'No. They drove my mum round to pick it up. They couldn't care less that I was missing. They just wanted the car away from the Bothy. It's in her garage, waiting for this nightmare to be over.'

'You've never heard from Jack again?' Chloe said.

Archie shook his head. 'Nothing. But then Davie Wylie came here looking for him and Henry. Then he went missing too.'

'Did you speak to Davie?' Harry asked.

'No. He spoke to my mum, but she gave him the same answer: I was missing. Then we read about him being missing.'

'What did you say to your mother about all of this?'

'I told her what had happened. She believed me when I showed her the photographs I took. I still have the photos, but I can't do anything with them. I mean, all they show is four men getting out of a black car – nothing that would stand up in court. But at least I have their faces recorded so I know what they look like. She confirmed it was the same men who came here looking for me.'

'Can you show me?'

Archie nodded, then left. He came back a few minutes later with his camera, a Nikon. He scrolled through the photos until he got to the ones that showed the men.

'Do you think I could take photos of those photos with my phone?' Harry asked.

'Yes, go ahead.'

Harry did.

'Harry, if you go looking for Jack and Henry, those guys will kill you.'

'We're not going to give up, son.'

'Do you live in your mum's attic all the time?' Chloe asked.

'Yes. I only come down into the house when she doesn't have any guests. But otherwise, I have my own bathroom and a large bedroom with a sitting area. I use headphones when I want to watch TV.'

'One more thing: what do you think of James Baxter?' Harry asked.

'Weirdo. My mum wanted me to get outside for some fresh air, so she thought it would be a good idea for me to go and clean the church. That lasted two weeks, then I disappeared. I didn't like him at all. I wouldn't have stayed working there.'

Harry took out his phone and wrote his number

down on a piece of paper. 'Call me if you can think of anything else.'

'It will have to be on the house phone. Or my mum's mobile. Mine is still active, to make it look like I can call home if I'm still alive. But I can't actively use it and it's switched off. I'll give you my mum's number though. She rarely uses her mobile.'

'Thanks for everything, Archie. Stay safe.' They shook hands.

TWENTY-SIX

Harry sat back in the car with his eyes closed for a few seconds. 'This Lord Corcoran seems like a real twisted psycho.' He opened his eyes and saw Chloe was crying again.

'What are we going to tell Lisa?' she said.

'We don't have to tell her anything just yet. What we heard was just somebody's account of what happened. I mean, Jack's never been found. Or Henry.'

Harry's phone rang. 'Hello?'

'Harry, it's Jimmy.'

'Hey, pal. How's things?'

'We're on our way and I'd like to have a few pints with the country yokels.'

'Smashing. What time will you be here?'

'Fifteen minutes out, son. Get the kettle on.'

'I look forward to it, Jimmy.'

Chloe had stopped crying. 'I'll be alright to drive,' she said, as if Harry had been slavering at the thought of getting behind the wheel.

'A couple of my friends are coming down this afternoon,' he said to her. 'You'll like them.'

'I'm sure I will.' She smiled a sad smile at him. 'Sorry I'm a wreck,' she said.

'We're all a wreck at one time or another,' he told her.

They drove back to their road. She parked in her driveway. 'Let me freshen up first, Harry.'

'You want me to come in with you?'

'No, I'll be fine. Tell the others I'll be up in a wee while.'

'Okay. Don't be long.'

Harry left her driveway and walked up the road to his house. Liam's van was still there. He'd told the old man to be careful and not go anywhere as it was too dangerous.

'Hi, Harry,' Lisa said. She was sitting on the floor with Alice, playing a game.

'Hi, Lisa. Where's Liam?'

'I'm through here, making tea. You want one?' the old man shouted from the kitchen.

'Aye, thanks.' Harry took his jacket off and sat down on the couch. 'My friends will be here shortly and they'll be wanting one too, no doubt.'

'How did you get on?' Lisa asked as Liam brought the tea through. Harry took the mug from him and sipped some of the hot liquid before answering.

'Davie Wylie's corpse was found at Loch Lomond today. He'd been buried in the graveyard next door, dug up and left on the shore.'

Lisa and Liam looked at him like they were waiting for a punchline that would never come.

'He went looking for Henry and somebody murdered him?' Lisa said, her face falling.

'I'm sorry, but yes, that's what it's looking like.'

'What about Jack and Henry?' Liam asked.'

'There was no sign, but that's a good thing,' Harry said. He didn't want to come right out and tell her about Archie's version of events, which involved Jack and Henry being hunted down by men with shotguns.

'You and I aren't stupid, Harry,' Lisa said.

He thought about fat ladies singing but kept quiet.

'Did you speak to Archie's mother?' Liam asked.

Harry stalled for a second, wondering if he

should tell them about talking to Archie, but he held back, one of the reasons being they might wonder why Archie had lived while Jack and Henry had died.

'Yes, I did. She didn't have anything to add that would help us.'

'Where's Chloe?' Lisa asked.

'She's in her house just now. She'll be up in a wee while. I think she's got a headache.'

They all looked up when they heard a car pulling into the driveway. Bella started barking at the door. Liam had a look on his face that suggested he was ready to go boxing. Harry approached the window and peered out through the net curtains. The original curtain-twitcher. He smiled when he saw who it was.

'Bella, that's enough,' Liam said, and the dog ran over to the corner, where she stood with her ears pricked up, looking at the door.

They all heard the raised voice.

'I could have driven a bloody tractor down here quicker,' Jimmy Dunbar said. 'Texting and driving, for God's sake. First of all, it's illegal, and second of all, can't you let Vern go for five minutes?'

'Yet here we are in one piece,' Robbie Evans said.

'A wing and a prayer they call it, son.' Dunbar smiled when Harry opened the door.

'Hi, Jimmy. Robbie.' Harry stood aside and let the two men in.

Bella growled, but Dunbar held out a hand and the dog sniffed it before wagging her tail and running away. 'Good girl,' Dunbar said. 'She remembers me.'

'Of course she remembers you,' Liam said. 'She only saw you a few days ago.'

Harry was puzzled by the comment, thinking the old man was confused.

'You're a sight for sore eyes, pal. I've changed my skids twice on the way down here,' Dunbar said to Harry.

Harry laughed. 'You never stop winding him up, do you?'

'Tell me he doesn't deserve it.' Dunbar put his suitcase down and shook Harry's hand, putting his other hand on Harry's upper arm. 'Good to see you again, pal.'

'You too, my friend.'

'We'll have a pint tonight. I need a wee refreshment.'

'Aye, me too.'

Dunbar let go and walked into the living room. Harry shook Evans's hand. 'Good to see you, pal.'

'You too, sir.'

Once they were inside, Harry was about to introduce his guests when Lisa ran over to Dunbar and put her arms around him. Then she started crying for a minute before pulling back.

'Thank God you're here, Jimmy.'

Dunbar nodded. Looked at Harry. 'I think it's time we introduced you properly to Harry. DCI Harry McNeil, meet Detective Inspector Lisa McDonald.'

TWENTY-SEVEN

Chloe more threw herself down onto her couch than sat down. It had been a hell of a day. To hear Archie Spencer say that Jack and Henry were dead had taken the wind out of her.

She was actually getting used to living here, but now she thought she would put the house back on the market. How could she stay here after this?

There was a painting on the wall that was one of her favourites, a little boy at the beach, the sun dipping down below the horizon. The boy was holding a bucket and spade, and he was wearing his little sunhat and a tee-shirt and shorts. It had been a great day.

If she had known what was going to happen three weeks later, she would have rushed over to the little boy and hugged him for all she was worth. As it was, she had taken a photo of him and walked over and taken him by the hand. It was only later on that she'd found the strength to make the photo into an oil painting.

She wished she could turn back the clock, to make one small change in her life that would have altered the course of history, but of course she couldn't.

He had been gone for ten years now. And every day for ten years, her heart had broken just that little bit more.

That was why the news of Henry dying had affected her so badly.

She had left Glasgow to find a place where nobody knew her. Where no friends would stop her in the street and ask how she was coping. How could she say she was coping with the death of her little boy? He was gone and nothing was bringing him back. So she had moved down here to Newton Stewart, to their little cottage where they would come with their son and spend a weekend. She would paint and they would kick back and enjoy the peace.

She wished she could bring him back so they could enjoy the time together again. But a drunk in a car had killed her son and messed up her husband.

Then he'd driven off and the police had never found out who he was.

Now, if she could do anything in her power to help somebody find a lost child, she would.

She got back up and went upstairs to freshen up.

And that's where the man was waiting for her.

TWENTY-EIGHT

Harry stood looking at Lisa for a moment, as if he had misheard Dunbar.

'Why don't we all have a seat and we can fill you in more, Harry,' Lisa said.

'I think I need a whisky,' Harry said. 'Liam, do the honours, please.'

'Aye-aye, Captain.' Liam scuttled away through to the kitchen to get some glasses.

'Sorry about the subterfuge,' Dunbar said, 'but let's get a seat and we'll explain.'

'That would be good,' Harry said.

They sat down and Liam came back in with the glasses and started pouring the whisky. Lisa refused. Alice sat on the carpet, playing.

'Where will we start?' Dunbar said.

'At the beginning,' Harry suggested. 'This should be good.'

'Lisa, you want to start?'

Lisa had the decency to look sheepish before she started talking. 'Let's go back a bit, before what happened last year,' she said. 'It involves Davie Wylie and Willie Munroe. I worked with them. When Jimmy introduced me as DI McDonald, he forgot to say *former* DI McDonald. I got fired last year. Except I wasn't.'

'That's what the force thinks,' said Dunbar. 'This goes way high up, Harry. It was made to look like she was fired. Technically, everybody thinks she was, but she's still on the payroll. Sorry, go ahead.'

'I was investigating Munroe and Wylie. We knew they were up to no good, but we weren't sure exactly what. Something illegal. Then my ex, Jack Easton, came to me one day and said he thought Davie Wylie was a hitman.

'I was taken aback, let me tell you. A hitman? I told Jack he was crazy, but he gave me names of people who had gone missing. He knew Willie Munroe was moonlighting for Lord Corcoran at the estate, and then he sent me photos of some men there. One was of Wylie holding a rifle. The other was of Willie Munroe holding a crossbow.'

'Davie Wylie had injuries that were made by a crossbow,' Dunbar said. 'Part of an arrow was stuck in his femur.'

'Jesus. They were hunting him?' Harry said.

'It looks like it,' Lisa said. 'But to get back to the story, Jack was using Henry to get close to whoever was on the estate. I think now that he thought it would look like less of a threat if he had a boy with him. Even a teenager.'

'That's what Archie confirmed.' They looked at Harry. 'Archie's not missing,' he went on. 'He's been hiding up in his mother's attic for a year, scared to come down in case the thugs kill him like they killed his friend Sarah.'

'He would have confirmed that Jack and Henry were at the centre?' Lisa asked.

'He did. He said they got captured.'

Dunbar took a sip of his whisky. 'That's why we had Lisa approach Wylie. By this time, we think Willie Munroe had tipped him off that he was being watched, so Wylie resigned. That caught us by surprise.'

'Even more so when we found out he had started a private investigation firm,' Evans said.

'So we got Lisa to approach him after Jack and Henry went missing, to see how he would react. To our surprise, he took the case, came down here, and disappeared just like Jack and Henry had. But we thought, why would he do that? Start a new life? Now we've found him dead, and it could be that Munroe had a hand in that.'

'How come you ended up here?' Harry asked Lisa.

Dunbar answered for her. 'I told her that a friend of mine had moved down to Newton Stewart. It was too good an opportunity to miss. I suggested she come down here. Lisa suggested bringing Liam and Alice.'

'That's a bit dangerous, don't you think?' Harry said to Lisa.

'I thought if I told you our story, you would offer to help, thinking that I didn't know you're a detective. Jimmy said your curiosity would kick in. It always does.'

'Don't you hate always being right?' Harry said to him.

'No, not really.' Dunbar grinned.

Harry looked at Lisa. 'Do you really live in the van?'

Lisa shook her head. 'No. I just made that up so you would feel sorry for us.'

'Mission accomplished.'

'And I'm not really one of Snow White's seven little friends,' Liam said, taking a sip of his whisky.

'What about when you told me you'd found Henry's phone in my fireplace?' Harry asked.

'Sorry, that was just a wee bit of embellishment. We'd been to the town before, but we were never in this house. Jimmy told us you'd bought this place. We did research and found the abandoned place up the hill from you on a map.'

'You all got me good and proper,' Harry said, no humour in his voice.

Dunbar's phone rang and he took it out of his pocket and looked at the screen.

'Sorry, I have to take this,' he said, getting up and going outside.

'Would Munroe have killed Wylie, do you think?' Liam said from his chair.

'I wouldn't put it past him. He uses his uniform to his advantage,' Lisa said.

After a few minutes, Dunbar came back in. His face looked grim as he sat down. 'This changes everything.'

'What is it, Jimmy?' Lisa asked.

'That was Dr Christie from the mortuary at the hospital. That body they have isn't Davie Wylie. It's Jack Easton.'

'Oh God,' Lisa said.

'And the girl who was dug up out of the grave too? Her name was Sarah Marshall, which I already knew. They're still waiting for the DNA results from their lab. Old Mrs Treadwell will be spinning in that grave knowing she was sharing it with two strangers.'

'Who?' Liam asked.

'That was the name on the gravestone where the two bodies were dug up,' Evans explained.

Harry looked at him for a minute, like he was trying to figure out the last clue of a crossword puzzle.

'Davie Wylie's still alive?' he said.

'Could be.'

'Is he married?' Harry asked. 'Any family members he could be hiding out with?'

'He was married a few years ago. They got divorced,' Lisa said. 'He didn't talk about her much. I only knew him for a couple of years and he was already divorced.'

'Do you think he went back to the estate?' Harry asked.

'I'm guessing they wouldn't be waiting with open arms,' Dunbar said.

'I didn't mean as a friend, Jimmy.'

'I know. If he's going back there, he'll be going to war.'

Harry chugged back his whisky. 'We should have a wee trip tonight. I'll call Archie and get directions. First, though, we should have a chippie for dinner.'

He got up and went through to the kitchen.

'Yay!' Alice shouted. 'Maisie wants some chips too.' She held up her toy cat for Jimmy to see.

'Does she, darlin'?' Dunbar said. 'Well, we'll just have to make sure she gets some chips then.' He smiled at the little girl and Lisa smiled at him.

'Thanks, boss.'

He smiled at her. 'She's a wee cracker, Lisa.'

'Jack didn't appreciate her, and now he won't ever be able to. Excuse me.' She got up out of the chair and rushed upstairs.

'Poor lassie. Jack was a bit of a heid the baw, but he was the bairn's father,' Dunbar said.

Harry came back into the room. 'Chloe isn't answering her phone. Maybe she's taking a nap. She was upset about Henry earlier. I'll call Archie. Can somebody call the chippie? They deliver. Here, use my card.' He handed Evans his American Express.

'Don't be calling up any sex lines with his card,' Dunbar said.

'As if. Besides, I have your card number for that.'

'I swear to God, if I see –'

'Relax, boss.'

They looked up the number and Evans went outside to dial it.

In the kitchen, Harry called Chloe's number but got no response. Then he called the other number he'd put into his contacts. Archie's mother's phone rang and he could hear the hesitancy in the younger man's voice as he answered his disposable phone.

'Hello?'

'Archie, it's me, Harry McNeil.'

'I thought you were Harry Mackay?'

'Listen, son, my name is Detective Chief Inspector Harry McNeil. I was here just kicking back and I didn't want anybody to know I was a copper. Now, I need your help. Can you draw a map of where we can look in this estate? My friends and I are going after dark.'

There was silence for a moment and Harry thought he'd been cut off. 'Archie?'

'I'll do more than that. I'll take you.'

'You don't have to, son.'

'I do. Talking to you today showed me that I don't have to live in hiding anymore. I'm sick of it. I'm going to take a stand. I'll come with you.'

'Good man. We're going to have dinner, so we'll leave when it gets dark.'

'It's not far, but it the roads are twisty.'

'Got it. I'll call you later.' He hung up and went through to the living room.

Evans came in. 'Chippie will be here in twenty.'

'I called Chloe but no answer,' Harry said. 'However, Archie is going to take us round to the estate.'

'We don't want to put him in any danger,' Lisa said.

'He's just going to show us where to go. Then he can leave,' Harry assured her.

They chatted for a little while, and then Harry decided to go down and knock on Chloe's door.

'I'll come with you,' Lisa said.

They put on their coats and walked out into the chill air. Darkness was creeping about like an old man in a dirty raincoat.

'I hope you're not pissed off at me, sir,' Lisa said.

'First of all, I'm not *sir*. I'm Harry, plain and simple. I don't know if I'm going back to that life of being a policeman.'

She stopped for a second on the stony road and looked at him. 'You know something, Jimmy Dunbar talks so highly of you, how you're a great copper. How you spent four years in Professional Standards.

You would have wiped the floor with Chief Inspector Willie Munroe. Then you were promoted to taking over a new MIT. Police Scotland would lose one of its best if you left, and I'm not just saying that.'

'Your concern is duly noted, Lisa.' He started walking again. 'Did Jimmy tell you anything else about me?'

She was silent for a moment before answering. 'Yes.'

'Care to elaborate?'

'He told me about Alex. How she died and you have a daughter who's five months old. You left her with your sister-in-law to get a break from it all, but you bought this house and haven't been back home since.'

'That's it in a nutshell.'

'Christ, Harry, don't you miss the bairn?'

He stopped so suddenly that she was taken aback for a moment. 'Of course I miss her, Lisa. Jesus Christ, I miss her every day. But what good am I to her? I'm almost forty-two. Her mother was thirty-two. Alex's sister is twenty-nine. That's young. She makes a better parent to the bairn, even though she's the auntie. I'm too old to bring up a wee girl. She needs a mum more than she needs a dad.'

'Really, Harry?' He was about to walk away

when Lisa stepped in front of him. 'Do you think my Alice didn't miss her dad? Jack was a tosser, plain and simple. He couldn't take it that Alice has Down's Syndrome, so he left. Irresponsible bastard. Yes, he gave me money, but she needed her dad. Now he's gone and she'll never see him again and I don't know if that makes me more sad or angry. Grace needs you. Yes, it's hard right now. You've been grieving. And yes, I'll grieve for the good times I had with Jack, but by God, if I meet somebody else, I'm not going to let those memories get in the way of my happiness. But with a daughter like Alice, they're hardly beating a path to my door.'

'What's your point?'

'Oh, don't be a smartarse. I'm sorry, you might be above me in rank, Harry, but this is a little girl we're talking about. A baby, no less. What did you run away down here for, so you wouldn't have to face up to your responsibilities?' Her eyes were wide now, tinged with tears. Her breath was coming fast.

'Grace and Jessica live in a big house, with a live-in housekeeper. All the bills are paid. They want for nothing. Jessica runs the nursery business I inherited.'

'So they have all the material things they need? Big deal. Grace needs her father.'

'I'm putting her up for adoption.'

'Like hell you are! I never met your wife, but I bet she would be smacking you around right now. Is that what she would have wanted? To have her daughter shoved away? Yes, there are fantastic families who will love a child, but it's nothing compared to being loved by a blood parent. You already have a bond with her. Go home and be with her, Harry. Leave this place and go home. Stop feeling so fucking sorry for yourself.'

She took a breath and blew it out. 'And if you want to reprimand me, then go ahead. I'm still on the payroll, as Jimmy pointed out.'

Harry's thoughts were buzzing about inside his head like a man who was pished riding the Waltzer.

'Let's go and knock on Chloe's door,' he said, his voice barely a whisper.

They walked past the little French electric car and up to her door. Harry knocked and rang the doorbell, but there was no reply. He saw a light on upstairs.

'She's probably fallen asleep. She looked worn out earlier.'

'Come on then, let's head back to the house.'

They started walking up the road again.

'Let me ask you something,' Harry said.

'Go ahead.'

'If I hadn't asked you, Liam and Alice into my house, what was your Plan B?'

'Never going to happen,' Lisa answered with a slight grin. 'Jimmy told me you would take pity on us and ask us in.'

'But what if?'

'Not in a million years.'

'Christ, Jimmy knows me better than I know myself.'

They went back inside and waited for the food to arrive.

TWENTY-NINE

Everyone was stuffed when they left the house.

'A quick beer in the Thistle before we go,' Harry said.

Once again, Chloe wasn't answering her phone or the knocking on her front door. Harry stared at Chloe's house as Lisa eased down the road.

'Maybe she took a sleeping pill,' Lisa said. She was behind the wheel in Dunbar's pool car. They had left Liam with Alice, and Bella was on guard duty.

Evans sat in the back texting Vern.

'You only saw her today,' Dunbar reminded him.

'We were supposed to have dinner tonight,' he said.

'She's hardly going to run off with the milkman because you came down here with me.'

'Oh, I don't know,' Lisa said, 'have you seen her milkman?'

Evans snapped his head up. 'Ma'am, please. You're just encouraging him. If you laugh at his jokes or respond to him in an affirmative manner, he'll never go away. And just wait till he's pished.'

'Wrap that, ya cheeky bastard. I know how to behave myself when I've had a couple of lager shandies.'

'Aye right. Shandies.' Evans went back to texting.

'Don't be sending her any of those...what do you call them again?' Dunbar said.

'Dick pics?' Lisa offered.

'Naw. I mean...emoji things.'

'Oh, right.'

'At least you've got the decency to pull a beamer,' Dunbar said. 'Dick pics. I'm sure that was the name of a comedian when I was growing up. He's probably in solitary now.'

They parked across from the Thistle and piled out into the darkness. They were about to cross the road when Harry put an arm on Dunbar's. 'See the licensee's name?'

'Aye.'

'The last name. Where did you just hear that name?'

'Christ.'

'Make a call and get somebody to do some research. Will your people still be at work?'

'They'd bloody well better be. I told them they're on overtime tonight. I'll call.'

He took his phone out and dialled a number. 'Tom? It's me, Dunbar.'

'I know, sir. Your name popped up.'

Dunbar was going to tell him that nobody liked a smartarse but kept it to himself. 'I want you to do a background check for me, son. Get Sylvia onto it too.' He told him what he wanted. 'Correct. I'll be in touch in a wee while. Is that other matter we discussed in hand?'

'Yes, it is.'

'Good. If this all goes tits-up, the buck stops with me. But don't get too comfy in my office chair just yet.'

'I wouldn't dream of it, sir.'

'Right. Get on with it and I'll call you back. Only call me if it's an emergency.'

They went into the bar. The usual suspects were there and they let on to Harry and looked at his friends. They would be dying to know who the others were, but Harry made no move to introduce them. He bought three pints and a glass of Coke.

'Scramble not on tonight?' Harry asked the barmaid, who he had seen in here many times.

'No, he's having a few days off.'

'Lucky him. He doing anything fun?'

'He doesn't tell me anything, Harry.' She poured the Coke and he handed over the money. 'Who are your friends? I haven't seen them before.'

'Just an old gang I used to hang out with.'

'Tell them they can come in here and spend their money anytime.'

'I'll pass that message on.'

He took the drinks over, making two trips, and sat down on a chair next to Evans while Lisa and Dunbar sat on the seat against the wall.

Harry took his phone out, inspired by Evans, and sent a text to Jessica. 'Grace okay?'

'Grace is fine. Maybe try calling her tomorrow? She'd love to hear Daddy's voice.'

'I will.'

Smiley face.

They chatted and it wasn't obvious that anybody was eavesdropping, but after one drink, they got up.

'Catch you later,' Harry said to the barmaid, who waved at him.

Outside, Dunbar took his phone out and called Tom Barclay while Lisa went over to start the car and get the heat going.

'Tom? It's Jimmy.' Dunbar put the phone on speaker and they listened while Barclay drew in a breath, about to remind him that his name had come up on his phone screen, but he saved it.

'I ran that name you gave me. Victoria Treadwell. Died in nineteen ninety. Old age. She had two sons, Max and Glen. Max was in the army; Glen is —'

'The licensee of the Thistle Hotel and bar in Newton Stewart.'

'That's correct. His brother, Max, is head of security for Lord Corcoran. He was a colonel in the army.'

'What about Davie Wylie? Did you trace any family?'

'He was divorced. They had a son, but he died. A drunk driver hit Wylie's car while he was driving and the son was killed. Wylie survived. The other driver took off and they never found him. Wylie got divorced not long after. This was ten years ago.'

'You get a name for the wife?'

'Annie Chloe Wylie. Records indicate that she went back to using her maiden name, Walker. She's now Chloe Walker.'

Dunbar thanked him and hung up as they ran over to the car.

'Boot it back to Chloe's house, Lisa,' Harry said. Dunbar told her what he'd found out.

Lisa screamed the car round and the journey took less than a minute. They stopped at Chloe's house and Harry ran to the front door and banged on it. He tried the handle and found the door was unlocked.

They all entered, splitting up. Harry ran upstairs and found a chair that had been at a dressing table in the middle of the large bedroom. There was duct tape on it, as if it had held somebody in place.

There was a note placed on it. Harry didn't have nitrile gloves, but he picked up the note anyway.

Come and get her, Davie. We'll be waiting. C.

'What you got?' Dunbar said, rushing into the room. He read it.

'Who's C?'

'Maybe Max Treadwell,' Harry said. 'He was a Colonel.'

'I think we know where the bastard twins are. I want those tossers, Harry. If they've killed young Henry, I'll rip the bastards apart.'

'Let's get Archie.'

They walked downstairs and out the front door.

'What about Liam and Alice?'

'They'll be well looked after,' Dunbar said as an armed response vehicle turned into the driveway and stopped.

'Next house up, son,' Dunbar said, showing his warrant card. 'The people we're after are armed and dangerous. Oh, and they have a wee dug in there.'

The car pulled up to Harry's drive. 'Better take two cars,' he said.

'I'll ride with you,' Lisa said to Harry.

'Okay,' he said reluctantly.

'Don't worry, I don't bite.'

'Trust me, that's not what I was worried about.'

THIRTY

The Autumn Bonanza was in full swing and Lord Corcoran was so excited, he was almost pissing himself.

'Once again, you're the centre of attention,' Colonel said.

'I am. I deserve it. Those mutants wouldn't be anywhere if it wasn't for me. But think of all the reciprocal invitations.'

Colonel could see the madness lurking there. This man lived for power, something he'd had since he was born. His father had encouraged it. Now the father was a shell of his former self, his mind having gone sideways with the cruel disease that was dementia.

'I want a whisky,' Senior said, coming into the

huge library they were now standing in.

Corcoran took a deep breath, composing himself. 'Dad, you know you'll piss the fucking bed if you drink this late at night.'

'I told him that,' said Phyllis, his nurse.

'I know. He's a stubborn old mule.' Corcoran turned to his father. 'Go to bed, Dad. You'll get a wee whisky tomorrow.'

'Och, I'll tell your mother and she'll skelp your bloody arse.'

'Goodnight, Dad.'

Phyllis led the old man out.

'Right, where were we?' Corcoran said to Colonel.

'The woman. Wylie's ex.'

'Oh, yes. That bastard is trying to ruin things for us. Do you think he burnt down the centre?'

'Without a doubt. Wylie was highly trained and now he's been slipped off his lead. He's running wild and God knows what he'll do. I think he torched the centre so nobody would be up there with telescopes and binoculars at this time. He's planning something big and he's been waiting for your bonanza to do it.'

Corcoran walked over to the drinks cabinet and poured them both a whisky. 'Do tell me again how you took care of him, Max.'

Colonel swirled the liquid around in the crystal glass. Would it be better to smash the glass and use a shard to kill the lord now, or just ride it out? He chose to sit down instead.

'It was when we grabbed those two last year, remember? That nosy reporter and his laddie.'

'Technically, his brother-in-law, but do go on.'

'We chased them and caught up with them. Davie Wylie was with the team...'

Colonel knew there was something up when he got the radio call that Archie Spencer was up at the centre. The little bastard was a trouble-maker, with all his shite about aliens and bases on the moon. He should have been put in the nuthouse a long time ago.

'Bravo One to Alpha Leader,' he heard Davie Wylie say over the radio.

'Go.'

'We're needed at the centre.'

'Copy. On my way.'

And that's what started off the night's events. Colonel going to the centre with a team. Archie Spencer, Jack Easton and Henry running for it. A team chasing Archie and finding the abandoned Land Rover at the roadside café. Wylie and Munroe and Colonel and another team going after the other two.

Easton and Henry ran. One of the team aimed his shotgun at Easton but missed. The boy was running in the opposite direction. Munroe had his crossbow and took a shot in the dark. They heard a scream, and Munroe grinned.

'That's how you fucking do it, ya fucking wee numpty,' he said to the guy with the shotgun.

Torchlight picked out Easton, and Munroe let him have it with another arrow. Then a third. One of the other men ran over and kicked Easton hard in the guts, and Easton expelled all the air in his lungs, unable to scream.

Munro had another arrow in his crossbow and took aim, but one of the team stepped forward, eager to get some of the action, and pulled the trigger on the shotgun, ending the chase for good. Munroe let go with the crossbow anyway. One of the arrows snapped in Easton's leg as it was being pulled out.

'Look,' one of the others said, dragging Henry through the woods in the dark. 'Wee bastard thought he could get away from me.'

Henry tried to scream when he saw his uncle

lying dead on the ground, but nothing came out. The man who had shot Easton turned his attention to Henry, who was standing on his own now.

Davie Wylie stepped in and shoved the shotgun up in the air just as the man pulled the trigger.

'What the fuck you doing, Wylie?' Munroe said, taking a step forward.

'What do you think I'm doing? He's a boy.'

'He's a fucking witness!' Munroe spat. Then he turned to one of the other men. 'Shoot the boy.'

Wylie took out a handgun and pointed it at Colonel. 'That's not how we fucking roll.'

Colonel looked uncertain now. The gears were turning in his head. 'Okay, you got your own way this time, Wylie.' He turned to the others. 'Take the boy to the usual place in the house. And this stays between us. Get rid of Easton in the usual place.'

Wylie held the gun on Colonel while the others walked away. 'He's just a boy,' he repeated.

When he was gone, Colonel turned to Munroe. 'Don't get too attached to him.'

'And that's when you told me you'd have an operative come up from London. One who works exclusively alone. No other team member would see him, he'd take care of Wylie and then he'd disappear into the night. I believe that's what you said, but do feel free to contradict me if I'm wrong.'

Colonel nodded. 'That is indeed what I said. I just got an obscure text, which was code for "the job's on". I wouldn't even see the guy. Wylie went back to his day job, but then he was back in Newton Stewart, asking questions. When I asked him what was going on, he said he had been hired by Easton's ex to look for him. He was going through the motions.

'Well, the next thing we know, Wylie is gone. Nobody asked about him and nobody talked about him. The operative was paid and I never heard from him again.'

'You never heard from your operative again because he was dead. Looks like Wylie dug up Easton and transported him to Luss, where he put him in a hole in the ground to make conversation with your mother. I have to say, that was very creative of Wylie to use your mother's grave.'

'I'm going to get very creative with Wylie when I see him next.'

'You seem very sure he's coming back,' Corcoran said.

'That's because I trained him. I know how he thinks.'

'Except you didn't think that he might be a better operative than your man from London. Or think that if he got the better of said operative then he might take the corpse and bury it where Easton was buried, swapping them round. You'd better go and find out for sure. Dig up Easton's grave. Besides Easton, he also put that dead girl in there as well. Sarah Marshall. This is what the Americans call a cluster fuck, Max. Unfuck it.'

Colonel squeezed the crystal glass to almost implosion point, but he didn't want to leave any blood behind. Not when some wee pimple-faced lassie in a lab could run a DNA test and put him away for life. Technology sucked sometimes.

'I will indeed. Wylie will be coming back here.'

'How can you be sure?'

'Because we left a message for him: if you want your ex-wife alive, then come and get her.'

'If it was my ex-wife, I'd be doing a dance if some bastard took her.'

'You don't know Wylie like I do. His ego is huge and I threw a challenge down to him. He'll come. Mark my words.'

'You'd better be right, Max.'

THIRTY-ONE

And Colonel *was* right. Davie Wylie had watched his arch-enemy's brother, Glen, leave the hotel and walk along to Annie's house. Or Chloe, as she was known now. Glen had taken his ex-wife and walked her down the road and into his car, which he'd parked at the side of the road.

Wylie couldn't give his position away, but he knew where Glen would be taking her. Once they were gone, he'd entered the house and found the note, taunting him.

Colonel knew Wylie would turn up. Not because Wylie had feelings for his ex-wife, but because he had thrown down the gauntlet. Would it be best if he just walked away? Of course it would.

But Colonel was going to pay for hiring that hitman who had failed in his job.

If they only knew that Wylie had been pulling the strings. He had been planning this for a year. This was going to be the last Bonanza that was ever held at the big house. He was going to make sure of it.

He was in one of the estate's luxury cabins, closed for security reasons when the Bonanza was on. These were luxury cabins, almost like extravagant sheds, and very comfortable inside. They also had a direct view over to the estate. A perfect line of sight if you were a trained sniper, like he was.

Now, like any good sniper worth his salt, he just had to sit back and wait.

THIRTY-TWO

Barlae was a dot on a map in Ayrshire, with nothing much going on year round. But for one week in September, it was transformed into a hub of activity, thanks to the Corcoran estate.

Archie Spencer had taken his old Land Rover out of his mother's garage and he hadn't felt so exposed once the two cars were following him. Now they were parked in the car park of an abandoned hotel in the centre of Glenluce, down the road from Barlae.

They were in the car park round the back of the police station, which was filled to capacity. Three ARVs with their armed response officers were parked ready to go. More vans had been drafted in. Marked and unmarked cars.

'This is as far as you go, son,' Harry said to Archie as they stepped out into the cold night air.

'Okay. I just wanted to come this far at least. Just to make me feel like I was a part of things.'

'You've done well. Is everything in place?'

'Yes. Back-up is there too.'

'You were a great help. Now, go into the police station where they'll keep you safe. There are armed officers in there.' Harry waved a uniform over and asked him to escort Archie inside.

A woman wearing a heavy jacket walked over to Dunbar. 'Jimmy, good to see you again.'

'You too, ma'am. Thanks for coming down here.'

'There has to be a superintendent in charge of an operation like this, and we should thank our lucky stars that Calvin Stewart is at Tulliallan.'

'Ma'am, this is DCI Harry McNeil who I told you about. Harry, this is Detective Superintendent Lynn McKenzie.'

'Pleased to meet you, ma'am.'

'I've heard good things about you, Harry,' she said as they shook hands. Then she looked around. 'I made some phone calls and we got this team together pretty quickly. After I mentioned who it was we were coming after. Lord Teflon. A lot of people would love to see him get what's coming to him.'

'He's a nasty piece of work,' Evans said. 'I was reading about him on the way down. People love him, though.'

'People tend to love others who will cover for their debauchery. If I thought my husband was going away for a business meeting like this, I'd tear him a new arsehole,' Lynn said. And by the look on her face, they believed her.

'Did the search warrants come through?' Dunbar asked.

'Yes. My team lead has them and he's going to execute them. The warrants, I mean, not Lord Snooty and his cronies.'

'Good. This is their bonfire night,' Dunbar said. He looked at his watch. 'It should be well alight now.'

'Then let's get mov–'

Her sentence was cut off by the first explosion.

THIRTY-THREE

Wylie knew it was easy to see the estate from the centre but taking a shot from there would have been virtually impossible. Not from the cabin, though. These luxury weekend cabins were so much closer. Into the dark would also have been impossible, but straight across from the cabins was the huge bonfire, lighting up the that area of the estate. It was well alight now and the privileged few were gathering round, drinking, laughing and no doubt mocking the less fortunate.

Wylie was about to change all that.

He followed faces through the scope. Then the man of the hour appeared and the sycophants cheered and clapped as their messiah walked towards the fire.

There was very little wind, and the conditions were perfect for the shot.

Colonel was standing beside Corcoran. He was next, but not a long-range shot for Wylie. No, his death was going to be up close and personal.

Wylie had the remote detonator by his side. But first, it was time to put Corcoran's lights out.

He took in a deep breath and held it, his finger caressing the trigger.

Then he felt the gun against the back of his head.

'You know I'll blow your fucking brains out, Davie,' Lisa McDonald said.

Wylie let his breath out. 'I know you will, Lisa.'

'You killed my ex-husband and my brother. Jack is no great loss. He was heading down a destructive path. But Henry. You sick, twisted fuck.'

'I saved his life.'

Lisa froze for a second. 'What?'

'They were going to shoot him in the face. I intervened. I couldn't save Jack, but I insisted on them taking Henry to the house. There are old cells down in the wine cellar. Colonel was raging, and he hired a hitman to take me out. I killed the hitman, and then I dumped Jack in the grave where Colonel's mother is buried in Luss. I also took the body of Sarah Marshall and put her in there too. They were buried behind the detached house on the property where Colonel lives. His back garden is a cemetery. It's where his victims are buried. The ground is so disturbed, he didn't notice that I'd taken Sarah Marshall out of the ground. I put Jack and her in the grave.'

'Why did you then dig them up at Luss and leave them on the shore?' Lisa asked.

'I wanted to send them a message. Rattle their cage. I knew Munroe would find out about it and alert Corcoran.'

'How do I know you're telling me the truth?'

'You don't.'

'Hand off the rifle. Slide it sideways.' Lisa's head was spinning now. What if he was telling the truth? Was Henry really still alive?

Wylie did as he was told.

'Good boy. Now, put your hands behind your back. I'm going to handcuff you –'

Wylie was quick, his special forces training kicking in like a reflex. He grabbed Lisa's gun and brought out his own gun, which had been hidden underneath him.

Lisa let out a grunt as he easily disarmed her. He got to his feet, towering over her.

'You should have let me take the shot. Doesn't matter, though. I have a Plan B.'

'What? Shoot me and carry on with what you're doing? Go ahead. Liam will look after Alice.'

'I'm not going to shoot you unless you make me. The choice is yours. Just don't do anything stupid, Lisa.'

'If it's revenge you want, let the courts deal with Corcoran.'

Wylie laughed. 'I wasn't trained that way. He's going to pay. He took Annie – Chloe, as you know her. I'm going to get her back. He's expecting me to come for her and I don't want to disappoint Colonel. He and I are going to look each other in the eye and one of us is going to die.'

'Davie, don't do this.'

'I have to go and get her. What I said about Henry is true. He's in the cellar. But you'll have to make a decision: try to arrest me or go save your brother. They're planning on putting him on a burning raft. I heard Colonel say that last year. When the boy turns eighteen, he's dead. It was his birthday the other day.'

'My colleagues have a search warrant. They're going in now.'

Wylie smiled. 'You don't understand. That warrant won't mean a thing. Here, let me explain.'

He took out the remote control device and pressed a button. The bonfire exploded into a thousand pieces, erupting like it was raining fire. People were thrown into the air by the force, and fire and burning wood hit everyone around. Then Lisa heard another explosion.

'That was Colonel's house. Now for the finale.'

This time, the big house in the distance on the estate erupted in fire.

'That fire is going to spread rapidly. Henry is in the wine cellar. You can stall here with me or go get him.'

'They're coming up the hill now, Davie. You won't get far.'

'I know they are. I can see them.' With both handguns in his pockets, Wylie stepped out of the cabin and looked through the scope, picking out the headlights of the ARV that was booting up the road. He opened fire several times and watched as the car left the road.

'Bye, Lisa. Give me a head start or I'll shoot you.'

Then he was gone, running through the dark towards the fire.

'Shots fired!' she screamed into her radio. 'Suspect is heading into the estate from the south. Explosions in the big house. Henry is in the basement! Bring everything you've got.'

THIRTY-FOUR

Lynn McKenzie heard the message come over the radio. 'Everybody move!' she shouted. The uniforms scrambled.

'Evans, go with an ARV up to the cabin. Harry, Jimmy, with me.'

They all jumped into their cars and Harry saw the fire engine kick into life. They had been joined by the retained firefighters from Newton Stewart, and another crew from Stranraer.

He and Dunbar were in their own cars and they followed Lynn along Main Street, down to the A75.

It only took them a few minutes to reach the estate. There was a barrier across the driveway. Nobody was in attendance at the guardhouse now, the explosions dictating that all hands be on deck.

Luckily, it was a wooden barrier and Lynn crushed it, ducking below the windscreen as the car hit it at high speed.

The line of vehicles followed. Some vehicles cut left to head up to the luxury cabins.

Harry saw there was chaos in the estate after the explosions. The bonfire was over to the left near the edge of the property line. It was still burning fiercely but scattered all over. He could see victims lying on the ground nearby. His lights picked out body parts, but his attention was on the main house now. Part of the top level was gone, and the fire was rapidly spreading below.

He pulled up away from the house to allow the fire engines in. Lynn McKenzie was over to one side and Dunbar pulled in.

'How many people live there?' Lynn asked.

'Twelve. The security staff live off-premises,' Dunbar said.

'Lisa said Henry is in the basement,' Harry said. 'That can only mean she spoke to Wylie.'

'Why would he tell her?' Lynn asked.

'She and Henry aren't part of the equation. He came here for Chloe. He gave Lisa a chance to save her brother,' Harry said.

'It was a good move,' Dunbar said. 'Give her a

choice: go and look for your brother or try and arrest me.'

'She made the right choice,' Harry said.

'We'll have to wait for the fire engines to get here before we can make an entry,' Lynn said.

Harry looked at Dunbar. 'If Henry's in the basement, he won't make it until the fire brigade get here. I'm going in.'

'Harry, no!' Lynn said.

Harry wasn't listening as he ran towards the front door of the huge house. The fire was at the opposite end of the building, ripping through it at a fast rate. Dunbar took off after him as more police cars pulled in and the first fire engine arrived.

Lisa came bursting out through the bushes and ran over to Lynn. 'I have to get to Henry!'

'Harry McNeil and Jimmy Dunbar just ran in. Lisa don't –' But it fell on deaf ears as Lisa ran into the burning building.

The fire engine stopped nearby. 'More are on their way from Ayr,' the commander told Lynn.

'I have three officers in there looking for two people. Henry, a teenage boy, and a woman. Chloe Walker's her name.'

The commander walked away to talk to his crew. Lynn prayed they weren't too late.

THIRTY-FIVE

Wylie had put a silencer on his handgun now. There were men running about, guests screaming and shouting, rushing past him to get out of the house.

'Christ, there's Wylie!' one of the two guards shouted, bringing up his shotgun.

Wylie shot him in the head at close range. The other one was going for a weapon inside his jacket, but he too died for his cause.

Wylie stepped over them and went through the door that led down to the old man's wine cellar. He heard shouting.

He took the steps quickly but quietly. At the bottom, he turned left. He knew where he was going and could do this blindfolded. The wine racks were lit up and the first person he saw was Old Man Corcoran.

'My chess player!' he shouted to Wylie.

Both of the guards, who were obviously on their way to execute Henry and Chloe, suddenly turned. Both were armed. Two rapid shots took them down, and Wylie walked over to them and put a bullet in each of their heads.

The wine rack that was a concealed door was open. He ran into the hallway that housed the cells. They were all open except one. He opened that door and looked in and saw Henry curled in a ball in the corner.

'Come out, son.'

Henry looked at him and Wylie held out a hand. He took it and stood up, and Wylie helped him out. 'You're going to be alright, but we have to hurry.'

'Where's Chloe?' Wylie asked the old man. Then a figure stepped into view, blocking his way.

'Wylie, you bastard!' Chief Inspector Willie Munroe said. 'You'll get what's coming to you. Both you and that useless cow Lisa-Fucking-McDonald.'

Wylie didn't say a word but let go of Henry's hand and punched Munroe in the gut. The big man doubled over and Wylie kicked him, watching his former boss fall in a heap. Then Wylie guided Henry out and shut the door. It could only be opened from this side.

After a few seconds, they could hear Munroe screaming.

'Where's the woman?' Wylie asked the old man.

'Not here. Colonel took her. He wants to play chess with her, obviously.'

'Took her where?'

The old man shrugged.

But Wylie knew. 'Come on, we have to get out.' He led Henry along the corridor, and then suddenly a figure was in his face.

'Lisa, for God's sake,' Wylie said.

'My colleagues are here. You won't get away.'

'This place is going to be filled with smoke soon. I'm trying to get Henry and the old man out.'

Henry looked at his sister and nodded.

'You can stand here and try and wrestle the gun out of my hand, or you can take your brother and get the hell out of here. Again, it's your choice, Lisa.'

Lisa's shoulders slumped. 'You're a bastard, Davie Wylie. But thank you.'

Wylie nodded and turned away. He knew there was a small stairway leading to the kitchen, so he turned the corner and disappeared from view.

Up at the top of the stairs leading into the main

hallway of the house, Lisa ushered Henry and Old Man Corcoran towards the front door.

Harry and Dunbar came running towards her.

'Did you see Wylie?' Harry asked.

'He was down there. There's no sign of Chloe.'

Then there was an almighty crash from upstairs and fire rained down on them.

THIRTY-SIX

Colonel's house was at the back of the main house, behind a copse of trees to keep it out of view. A carriage house many years before, it had been converted. It had a triple garage over to the left and a Land Rover was parked in front, a pick-up model with a canvas roof. Another one was parked next to it, a normal vehicle, short wheelbase. The carriage house itself was well alight, sparks and flames dancing into the dark air.

Wylie walked as close as he could get to the house, his gun by his side.

Colonel stepped out from behind the second vehicle. 'Drop the gun, Davie.'

He was holding a gun to Chloe's head.

Wylie threw the gun away into the darkness.

'Step over here where I can see you better,' Colonel demanded. The flames from the house threw light out into the courtyard.

'Just let her go, Colonel.'

'Now, what would be the fun in that?'

'It's me you want, not her. Just let her walk and you can kill me at your leisure.'

Colonel roughly pushed Chloe away from him. 'Maybe I'll just shoot you both.'

Wylie eased closer to the pick-up. Colonel walked forward, ignoring Chloe but keeping his eye on her.

'You're a loser, Wylie. I tried to give you a chance, but your kid dying in that crash made you soft.'

'Don't you dare talk about our son like that!' Chloe spat.

'Oh, shut up. I only brought him on board because I felt guilty.'

'What do you mean, guilty?' Wylie asked.

'They never did find the drunk driver, did they?'

It was a question that neither Wylie nor Chloe had to answer because they knew. The man who had accidentally run Wylie off the road had driven off.

Colonel kept the gun on them but reached behind him and opened one of the double doors to the garage. They could make out the shape of a car inside.

'This is my brother's car. It's sat in here for over ten years. Ever since the night he hit you. Yes, it was Scramble who hit you and left. Mind you, he did stop to have a look first, but he saw the boy was dead. He called me and I told him to drive here. To be honest, he thought you were both dead.'

Colonel turned to shut the door, and something deep inside of Chloe exploded and she screamed and ran at him. He turned and swiped his gun across her face and she fell to the ground.

'Stupid bitch,' he said and pointed the gun at her.

Seeing his ex-wife run at Colonel, Wylie had reached into the back of the pick-up and grabbed the crossbow. No warning given, he just picked up the weapon, aimed and fired. Just like Colonel had taught him.

The arrow shot into the side of Colonel's head, right through his ear, severing his brain stem. He was dead before he hit the ground.

Wylie walked over to Chloe, who was standing crying, her shoulders shaking. She picked up Colonel's gun, and only then did she see the movement.

She didn't have time to shout a warning as

Scramble got out of the pick-up, grabbing another crossbow from the back. He was halfway to raising it when Chloe pulled the trigger, hitting the man in the face.

Wylie jumped round when he saw she had fired the gun. Scramble fell down dead, the crossbow falling from his hands.

'Aim for centre mass, I always taught you.'

'I did,' Chloe said.

Wylie gently took the gun off her. 'It's over now.'

'You need to go. They'll be coming here to check it out. The keys are in that small Land Rover. Go, Davie.'

'I never stopped loving you, Annie.'

'I know.'

'This is it. I have to disappear for good.'

She nodded. 'Just go.'

'Have a good life, Annie,' he said, getting behind the wheel. He reversed out of the garage and drove round the garage block. He knew where to find the tracks that the small SUV could follow through the woods. He kept the lights off and was swallowed by the darkness.

Chloe Walker would never see Davie Wylie again.

THIRTY-SEVEN

Harry jumped into Lynn's car, then she booted it round to the burning house at the back. Her headlights picked out the woman running towards them. She jammed the brakes on and the car skidded to a halt on the gravel driveway. It was Chloe Walker.

'Colonel's dead. So is Scramble, his brother,' she said as Harry ran forward. She threw herself into his arms.

'Is Wylie here?'

'I didn't see him.'

Lynn got out of the car and saw the two bodies lying in the courtyard, the corpses' shadows dancing in the light from the raging fire. There was another explosion and burning debris blew out onto the pickup. It went up in flames in what seemed like seconds.

'Jesus, get in the car,' Lynn said. Chloe and Harry got in the back and she spun the car round and headed back, keeping away from the main house.

'Did you get Henry out?' Chloe asked, panic in her voice.

'Yes, he got out.'

'What happened with Colonel and Scramble?' Harry asked.

'Colonel was holding me, keeping his gun out. He was convinced Wylie was going to come for me. He wanted to use me as a shield. The big house was well alight, and Colonel's house too. Scramble was getting antsy. He said he didn't want to wait for Wylie and that they should kill me now. I was shaking so badly. Then Scramble lifted the crossbow from the back of that truck and aimed it at me. I thought I was going to die, Harry. His aim was way off and the arrow hit Colonel in the side of the head. When he fell down, I grabbed his gun and Scramble was trying to reload, so I shot him. Then you appeared.'

'God knows where Wylie went,' Lynn said. 'Maybe he didn't make it out of the big house.'

'We'll find out soon enough,' Harry said.

He got out of the car and stood beside Dunbar and Evans.

'There's no sign of Wylie,' he said.

'I figured. Maybe it was too risky for him to come back for his ex. Or maybe he died in the fire. Either way, good riddance. If he left, I doubt we'll ever see him again. He's trained to disappear.'

'Aye, he's good at escape and evasion,' Evans said.

Harry didn't mention the small dark Land Rover he'd seen booting it away behind the garage block.

THIRTY-EIGHT

Three days later

'I'm going to miss the Thistle,' Chloe said to Lisa.

'You're moving up to Edinburgh. There are plenty of pubs there too.'

'I know. But we had a laugh, didn't we?'

'We did.'

The removal men had finished emptying Chloe's house, including her paintings, and the driver honked the horn as he gingerly drove down towards the main road.

'Well, there goes your stuff,' Liam said. 'You'll never see that again.' Bella barked her agreement.

'Grandad, for goodness' sake,' Lisa said. She had

her arm around Henry's shoulders. 'I got a call from Jimmy this morning. They found Jack's car in one of those garages.'

'They're still going through the property. They haven't confirmed Lord Corcoran's death yet, he was so messed up. It'll take a wee while to identify him,' Harry said.

'Jimmy also said the lab reports came back and the DNA from underneath Sarah Marshall's fingernails belonged to Colonel.'

'Jesus. Everybody will be distancing themselves from that family now,' Liam said.

'They found Willie Munroe dead in the cellar. Smoke inhalation,' Harry said.

'Grandad, take Henry and Alice into the house. I want to have a word with Harry for a moment.'

'I'll go and get the kettle on,' Chloe said, taking Alice's hand. Harry's house was empty too, except for tea- and coffee-making paraphernalia.

'I just wanted to thank you for all you've done. I'm sorry about all the subterfuge,' said Lisa.

'Don't worry about it. I was getting bored anyway.' Harry smiled at her. 'I listened to what you said. About feeling sorry for myself. I needed that kick up the arse.'

'I'm glad I could help. Both houses going on the market tomorrow?'

'They are indeed. It feels good to be going home.'

'You need this, Harry. I only yelled at you because I'm a mother.'

'I know. It's what Alex would have wanted.'

'And you'll look after Chloe?'

'I will. The house I have is big. She can stay with me and Jessica and Grace and the housekeeper for as long as she wants. I'll help her set up an artist's studio.'

'If you ever need me, just give me a call.'

'I will.'

Inside the house, Alice came running over to him. 'Can we play dolls?'

'Of course we can, sweetheart. Of course we can.'

THIRTY-NINE

'This is a big house,' Chloe said as Harry got out of his car. She locked her own car.

'This is the house that was left to me. Come on in, let me introduce you to Jessica and my daughter.'

He walked up the front steps, past leaves being blown about in the chill wind.

The front door was unlocked. He stepped into the house, and the memories – good and bad – hit him like a hammer, and he suddenly had a longing for Newton Stewart.

'This is so nice,' Chloe said, bringing him back.

'It's a beautiful place. Come on in.'

They put their bags in the hallway and went through to the living room. Jessica was sitting in a chair and she smiled at him as he came in. Grace was on the floor, playing with toys.

'Hi, Jess,' he said. She stood up and walked over to him and put her arms around him.

'It's so good to have you back, Harry.'

'It's good to be back. Jess, this is my friend Chloe, who I told you about.'

'Nice to meet you, Chloe.'

'Likewise.'

Jessica had the TV on and Harry could see it was tuned to a news channel. It caught his eye, but he went over to Grace first. He bent down and she started crying.

'Oops,' he said.

Jessica picked her up. 'She hasn't seen you in a while. She'll get used to you again. Just give her a wee bit of time.'

'I understand.'

He turned his attention back to the TV and picked up the remote from the arm of a chair.

'*...and police confirmed today that the badly charred corpse of Lord Corcoran has been positively identified through DNA. The cause of the explosion at the house has not yet been determined, but foul play is the most likely answer. Now, over to Andrew at the site.*'

The screen switched to a reporter out in the field.

'Thank you, Mary. Police this morning said that the cause of the explosions in the main house and the smaller carriage house is still being investigated. However, police search teams have uncovered more bodies behind the carriage house. That takes the count to seventeen that have been dug up, leading to speculation that somebody living on the estate was a mass murderer...'

'Corcoran got off lightly, if you ask me,' Chloe said.

'I don't think he would have taken to prison,' Harry agreed. Then he turned his attention to Grace again. This time she smiled at him.

'Are you going to, Daddy?' Jessica asked.

Grace put her arms out and Harry took her. He knew then for certain that his daughter wasn't going anywhere else. He held her tightly for a moment, putting his head next to hers. 'I love you, Grace McNeil.'

AFTERWORD

Here we are again, at the end of the road with Harry McNeil. I hope you enjoyed this journey.

We, as writers, make up stuff for a living, in fiction books, and this book was no different. The Corcoran estate is not based on any real estate but merely a figment of my imagination. The Galloway Wildlife Centre doesn't exist either.

The houses on Harry's road don't exist, only the road itself. For those of you who haven't heard of Bohemian Grove, it does exist.

And, of course, Bella really exists. These days, she lies under my desk during the day, napping, keeping me company.

And now, just a few people to thank. My wife as usual, for tolerating me at times. You're the best! To

RL for helping me with some research. To Jacqueline Beard – an amazing lady. A huge thanks to my editor, Charlie Wilson.

To all the new readers who asked to be on my advance team – welcome aboard. If you fancy joining them, message me on Facebook, John Carson Author. It's free and you get a free copy of each new book that comes out, and your email will never be given out to anybody else. Trust me, I'm a doctor. I mean, writer.

Thanks to Julie and Wendy for sticking with me on this journey. A lot more stations to go before we reach the terminus. Thank you to my niece Lynn McKenzie. Thanks to you, the reader, for making all of this worthwhile.

And last but not least, a huge thanks to the real Lisa McDonald for letting me use her name for a character. It was a blast!

Stay safe, my friends.

John Carson
New York
October 2021

Printed in Great Britain
by Amazon